ROGUE GENTLEMAN

KYLIE GILMORE

First Edition: January 2020

Cover design by Michele Catalano Creative

Published by: Extra Fancy Books

ISBN-10: 1-947379-23-2

ISBN-13: 978-1-947379-23-7

Love in very close quarters...

1

———

I'm a proud man, ambitious too, which is how I got myself into this predicament. On top of my day job, I'm on a tight deadline to finish renovating the old brownstone in Brooklyn where I used to live with my ex. Now it's just me, living and working here. I climb the steps and pull my key out. God, I'm tired. It's midnight and I'm jet-lagged from the long flight back from Villroy, where my older brother, Dylan, had his wedding. I just need to finish the renovation and things will ease up.

I step inside the empty living room, leaving my suitcase by the door, and turn on the flashlight on my phone. Overhead lighting isn't hooked up on this level. *Cre-e-eak.* I freeze, suddenly alert. A door just opened *inside* the house.

I listen intently. Someone is moving around downstairs. I turn off the flashlight and tuck my phone in my pocket, stealthily making my way downstairs just as someone flops down on the couch in the den. An intruder is making themselves comfortable on my couch? What the hell?

I flip the lights on.

"Ah!" a feminine voice squeaks. She jackknifes upright.

I stride over to her. "Who're you?"

She's young, twentysomething, her red hair in a messy

knot on top of her head, wearing a white top with a big Smokey the Bear face. She scrambles off the couch, grabs her phone, and stands a distance away. Her red pajama shorts sport tiny bear faces. Definitely not thief material in those pajamas. She's cute, but who cares? She's an intruder.

"Who're you?" she demands, holding up her phone with a finger hovering over it. "I have nine-one-one on speed dial!"

I stifle a groan. There's a shortcut for an emergency dial, but I'm not going to share that. "I live here. Who're you, and what're ya doing here?"

She lowers her phone. "You're the contractor? No, forget I said that." She raises her phone again, her finger hovering threateningly over it. "Now you're just going to agree that's who you are when you're probably here to rob the place."

I shove a hand in my hair. I'm too tired for this shit. "There's nothing here to steal unless you want to haul off some construction supplies and sell them on the black market. I'm Sean Rourke, the contractor for Winnie Abbott's place. Now, who the hell are you?"

She lowers her phone to her side, muttering to herself. I only catch "big old grump."

I step closer, and her blue eyes widen. I halt. I'm not trying to scare her. I just need to know who she is and what she's doing here. Then I realize I only need one thing. "You need to leave."

"I'm Winnie's cousin, Josie Abbott." At my silence, she adds, "Your new roomie. She said I could crash here."

I blink. "Roomie?"

She gives me a small smile. "Yeah. Winnie told me you were living here during the renovation. I was just surprised because you don't look like I thought based on her, um, description."

My brain stalls and then cycles through everything wrong with this situation—

I have six weeks to finish this renovation.

This week is critical. I took time off my day job to make progress here.

An unwanted guest is going to be a huge inconvenience.

"Goodnight, roomie," she says and slips under a pale pink fleece blanket on *my* couch. It's the only piece of furniture in the place and it's mine. I made it myself.

Why didn't Winnie tell me her cousin was moving in?

I pivot on my heel, pissed but too tired to deal with this right now. I slap the light off on my way upstairs, make my way to my air mattress, strip down to my boxer briefs, and collapse in bed.

I wake to the sun streaming in through the large drop cloth I put up as a makeshift curtain. Bleary-eyed, I head downstairs to the only functioning bathroom in the house and halt in my tracks. Crap. I forgot about her. Josie, my unwanted guest. Of course she's hogging the bathroom, brushing her teeth with the door wide open.

She's bending over the sink in her snug red pajama shorts with tiny bear faces all over her fine ass. Hell. Now I have to pee *and* I'm getting turned on. Bad combo. I shift my gaze, taking in toned legs and bare feet. Still turned on.

I stare at the ceiling, thinking cooling thoughts. Any woman in snug pajama shorts would be appealing. I haven't had time to date lately, working two jobs. The real problem is there's a small amount of livable space here—the place is a construction zone—and now I have to share it with *her*. I can't even kick her out because it's Winnie's place.

I take in her red hair up in a ponytail, the delicate line of her neck, her white long-sleeved pajama top with red trim —*Stop looking!*

"Can ya hurry up?" I grumble.

She glances back at me, her gaze dropping to take in my bare chest and boxer briefs before returning to my eyes. Seeming unconcerned by my grumbling, morning wood, or my lack of clothes, she holds up a finger to wait and points to her toothbrush.

I grit my teeth. I consider going upstairs to throw on a T-shirt and jeans, but who's the intruder here? Besides, I have more urgent concerns, like peeing and getting back to work. Ya know, it's just like Winnie to forget to tell me her cousin would be crashing here. She was never one for practical details, always dreamy, her head in the clouds. I used to think it was ideal how we balanced each other out. I'm the steady, responsible one; she's the dreamy, domestic one. Then she dreamed her way to a different life with a Wall Street guy. He's the one pressuring her to sell this place in a hurry, which is why I'm dealing with a too-tight deadline on the renovation. When she walked out on me to go live with him, she swore she hadn't cheated. It was an affair of the heart, not the body. I'm over it.

Josie finishes brushing her teeth and straightens. Our eyes meet in the mirror of the medicine cabinet. Her blue eyes sparkle like she has something fun she wants to share with me. I just know she spells trouble.

She turns to me with a big smile that's like a thousand sunbeams suddenly shining on a cloudy day. "Hi!" She lifts a hand in a little wave. "Last night was a little weird. Let's start over." She offers her hand. "I'm Josie Abbott. Nice to meet you." At my silence, she adds, "Winnie's cousin." Like I could forget. They have the same last name.

"Why didn't ya crash at Winnie's place in the city?"

She crinkles her nose. "It's a one-bedroom apartment, and I didn't want to intrude on their love nest."

Love nest? Barf. I keep that to myself because all I care about is this major wrench in the works.

She looks up at me expectantly like I might have more questions. It occurs to me she looks nothing like Winnie, which could mean Josie really is an intruder. Like a con woman. I'd be within my rights to kick her out, then.

"You don't look like Winnie." My ex is blond with rounder cheeks and a nose that turns up at the end. Josie's nose is straight and her cheekbones are high and prominent. My hopes rise on the eviction angle. "I'll need to see ID."

She rolls her eyes and pulls the ponytail band loose. Her red hair cascades over her shoulders in a tousled look that makes my mouth go dry. "I'm blond like Winnie, but I dye my hair red to stand out from the herd. Very important in my profession."

"Which is?"

"I'm an actress."

She's one of those too-good-looking people on TV, or maybe the movies. I don't recognize her from anything though.

She snaps her fingers in front of my face. "Still there?" She glances at my crotch, her cheeks flushing pink. "Do you want a towel or something?"

"I'm fine." *Let her look.* And look she does, her gaze making a slow trail up my torso, lingering on my chest before finally landing on my shoulder and bicep. I keep fit, and I'm not modest about it.

I snap my fingers in her face. "Still there?"

Her gaze meets mine calmly, her voice smooth and even. "Maybe we should work out a bathroom schedule."

"Maybe you should show me your ID."

"I'm not done getting ready. I'll show you after. Geez." She holds up a finger. "Okay, here's something only Winnie's cousin would know: when she has a nightmare, her eyes open and she speaks gibberish, even though she's still asleep. Freaky cousin sleepover fun!"

Damn. Winnie does do that, and it's like something out of a horror movie.

I slam my hands on my hips. "I don't know why Winnie sent ya here. It's not livable. There's only one functioning bathroom—" I gesture behind her "—and it's a powder room with no shower. The kitchen will be demolished soon, and there aren't any beds."

She lifts one shoulder up and down. "I can shower at the gym, and I'm fine with the couch. I've been crashing on friends' couches for months while I auditioned for pilot season in LA." She cups her mouth with one hand like she's about to share a secret, her voice lowering conspiratorially. "I have to use what money I have for traveling to auditions and classes to keep me sharp and marketable." She bounces on the balls of her feet, a smile tugging at her lips. "Got one too."

"One what?"

"A pilot! You're looking at the future lead of a soon-to-be-announced sitcom." She puts her hands on her hips, one leg bending in a red-carpet pose. "My big break! I can't tell you the name of it or what it's about, but it's going to be epic." She throws her arms up in a V of victory. I suspect she was once a cheerleader. I am *not* imagining high kicks in a short skirt.

I tear my gaze away from her. *Focus.* My ex's cousin is an out-of-work actress crashing on *my* couch. Not that it matters that she's claiming the only thing that's mine besides my stupid air mattress. The real issue is that I have to share close quarters with her, and I can already tell she's going to be a huge distraction with all her good cheer. Maybe Winnie didn't forget to tell me about this unwanted visitor. Maybe she sent her here purposely to distract me, hoping I'd fail at my deadline, which would make it easier for her to feel justified in hiring someone to replace me. A devious plan I refuse to fall for. We have a deal. This is *my* project.

Priorities. Nature calls. "I need the bathroom. Alone."

"Gotcha."

She brushes past me, and I catch the sweet scent of something fruity and floral. How can she smell so good first thing in the morning?

Finally, I get the bathroom to myself. I lock the door and take care of business, letting out a long breath of relief. Her voice carries through the door like she's standing right next to me. *Boundaries, woman!*

"I hope it didn't sound like I was bragging," she says. "It's not actually a done deal for the pilot. I'm waiting to hear if it's picked up by the network. I have a good feeling about this one though, so that's something. I'm moving out to LA the moment I hear it's picked up. Have to think positive!"

She's one of those annoying morning people. It's easier to be irritated when I'm not looking at her. I don't think I've ever seen another woman so effortlessly beautiful, with messy hair, no makeup, and ridiculous Smokey the Bear pajamas. She has that "it" factor that makes someone light up the screen. I'm sure she'll be out to LA very soon.

I wash my hands and give myself a stern lecture in the mirror. *You can do this. Keep it civil and get the work done.*

I was raised with excellent manners due to my royal father. If my dad hadn't abdicated the throne, he would've been king of Villroy, which makes me a prince. Not that I had any kind of wealth or privilege growing up in a working-class neighborhood in Brooklyn. He abdicated the throne to marry my mom, a commoner, and was exiled with nothing but the shirt on his back. In any case, the manners come in handy with women. Winnie used to love calling me a gentleman. She even upped my classy gentleman status by adding pricey clothes to my wardrobe, which was fine by me. I aspire above my paygrade. There's that ambition.

"Can I come in?" she asks. "I heard you flush and wash hands."

I blow out an exasperated breath. I can handle any woman, even an unwanted roommate.

I open the door, and Josie smiles up at me, looking way too cheerful.

"This is not gonna work," I growl. "I don't know what the hell Winnie's thinking having a guest here in the middle of a renovation. I've got work to do!"

Josie doesn't take my warning growl to heart, apparently, because she joins me in the small space of the bathroom and pulls her brush out of the medicine cabinet, brushing out her long hair. I carefully step around her.

She stills, brush in hand. "Winnie says she's tired of your grumbling. I kinda see what she means."

I halt my retreat. "If I'm grumbling, it's only because she suddenly made an outrageous deadline before she puts this place on the market."

She gives me a pointed look. "From what I understand, you're staying here for free."

"It's not free!" I rarely lose my temper, but this is an extreme circumstance. She's getting all up in my business!

I work for an even tone. "It's an *exchange*. I live here while I renovate it. She gets free labor from an experienced contractor. You can't find a better deal anywhere." And I really want to live in this upscale neighborhood, Park Slope, instead of a studio apartment somewhere I can afford. Park Slope is right by the park, only forty minutes to the city, and has a laid-back vibe with a lot of families and creative people living here. I keep hoping something will come on the market in my price range. Maybe another fixer-upper, though there's few left in this neighborhood.

Her brows pull down, her blue eyes sympathetic. "Are you still mad about Winnie getting engaged so fast?"

"No. I was never mad. We broke up ten months ago. It's ancient history."

She goes back to brushing her hair. "That's good. I have to say she's really happy. She never said a word about you to me while you two were together, so it must be the right match with Colin. She can't shut up about him. Obviously, there's no hard feelings between you two, right? I mean, since you're still working here at her place. You must be one of those enlightened men. That's nice."

I'm irritated again. Beyond irritated, and I don't know if it's because of her or Winnie. Maybe both. "We lived together for six months and she never said a word about me?"

Her eyes widen. "Did I say the wrong thing? I'm sorry. I thought—"

"Forget it."

She sets her brush in the medicine cabinet and turns to me. "Maybe she didn't mention you because she and I were both so busy at the time." She nods once. "Yes, I'm sure that's what it was. I was probably hustling to auditions and classes, and she was commuting to the art gallery, so…forget I said all that. Can we start over?" She steps closer and smiles her big sunshine smile. "Hi!" She offers her hand. "I'm Jo—"

"I'm gonna call Winnie."

But first I need to get clean after the long day of travel yesterday. I turn and head out the back door for the outdoor shower. I didn't mention it to Josie because I was trying to make this place sound as unappealing as possible. Normally, I shower at the end of the workday when I'm covered in sweat, and it's cooler on this mid-April morning than I'd like for a shower, but I need the space to myself and the refresher. I head through the garden, straight to the wooden shower stall tucked behind some climbing rose trellises. I set my briefs on the bench just outside it and step into the privacy of the shower, standing to the side while I turn the water on, giving it a chance to warm up.

"You keep your phone outside?" she calls from the back deck. Her voice must carry to the last row of a theater and definitely carries to the entire neighborhood.

If I ignore her, she'll go away.

The water warms, and I step under the spray.

"Do you hear water flowing like rain?" she calls. "Is that a fountain?"

I stick my face in the spray, closing my eyes. *Please go away.*

It's quiet for a few moments, so I relax.

"Oh!"

I whirl, and she's standing right there, staring. *Everywhere.*

"Go away!" I bark.

"Sorry!" She turns on her heel and walks swiftly back toward the house. "I didn't know there was an outdoor shower!"

I let out a breath and reach for the shampoo. I can't relax until I know she's back inside.

"Now I *really* feel like we have to start over again!" She sounds closer, like she's heading back toward me.

I scowl and scrub the shampoo into my hair. I swear if she comes back here and offers her hand to shake in yet another introduction, I'm going to do something I regret. Like yell at her, and then she'll go crying to Winnie, who'll go from impatient with me to enraged. Forget finishing the renovation. Winnie will kick me out and replace me with another contractor. I love this old house, and I've put in so much work here already. I started the renovation back when Winnie and I were together, with a shared vision to bring this run-down gem back to its former glory. It's from the 1880s, a twenty-foot-wide four-story townhouse with high ceilings and southern exposure, which brings in lots of light and makes it feel roomy. Before we broke up, I put in this garden and outdoor shower; plus I redid the roof and windows. I want to see it through. I want the pride and satisfaction of seeing this place restored. This is bigger than Winnie. Bigger than Josie. This is about me and my skill in restoring this historic beauty.

I glance at the bench, where I left my briefs, and realize I forgot my towel. Shit.

"You still there?" I ask.

Silence.

"Josie?"

"Um, yeah. Heading back inside now!"

I speak through my teeth. "Can you please get me a towel from the large duffel bag upstairs? It's by my air mattress."

"You sleep on an air mattress? The couch has got to be more comfortable—"

"Towel!"

"Right!"

I shift so I can see when she gets to the back deck. The moment she gets there, she stops and calls to me in her loud theater voice, "We'll take two—or is it three or four?—on the intros once you're dressed!"

I shake my head and tip it back in the spray. I am so screwed.

2

Josie

Well, this is an inauspicious beginning. Since when is there an outdoor shower in Grandmom's backyard? I find the duffel bag and pull out a thick blue towel. Sean Rourke, an actual prince. Winnie mentioned it when she offered to let me crash here, and I saw all the media buzz about his family reconciling with the royal family in Villroy. His older brother, Dylan's wedding this past weekend was a big deal. It was the first time someone on the exiled side of the family was married in the royal chapel. I caught glimpses of the wedding on the news on my flight out here.

Winnie says Sean's been here since she moved out. Ten months on an air mattress with a couple of duffel bags? Not exactly what you'd expect from a prince. He's worse than me, crashing on friends' couches. Actually, they weren't all friends of mine. I found this app called Couch Crasher, which is a network of actors looking for a free couch for a short stay. My last couch in LA was a bad experience. It was at a woman's apartment, but she had this giant skeeze of a boyfriend and, when she stepped out to get him beer, he propositioned me. I said no, and then he got a predatory look in his eye that sent chills through me. He took one menacing step toward me, and I turned and ran to my only available escape—the bedroom. I locked the door and pushed the dresser against it. He pounded on the door so hard I swore it would splinter.

I dialed 911 with shaking hands, ignoring the vicious insults he was shouting at me. The cops arrived at the same time as the woman who lived there. I made it out safely and called Winnie, telling her the harrowing story. She's six years older than me and always felt more like a supportive big sister than a cousin. She insisted I quit the Couch Crasher app, which I would've anyway after that, and invited me to stay with her and Colin. I really didn't want to intrude on them. And, honestly, Colin is one of those rigid uptight guys who make me tense.

Anyway, Winnie then told me I could crash on the couch at our grandmother's former place in Brooklyn. It seemed ideal. Brooklyn is cool, and I could commute to the city for auditions and to visit Winnie. She did warn me about Sean, saying he was a big old grump, but also a complete gentleman, and it would be like having a security guard around here. Her exact words to describe the grump? An older, protective sort of man with a sense of honor. Winnie's thirty, so I was picturing a grumbling, middle-aged guy in droopy dad jeans. She must've meant older than me. I'm twenty-four. Young hot guy took me by surprise.

I don't mind a little grumpiness as long as I can finally let go of the jumpy scared feeling that I'm suddenly going to be chased down by an aggressive man again. I'm not sure if it was Winnie's description of Sean as protective or just his natural presence, but I immediately felt safe with him. This is a man who'll watch your back for you.

I head downstairs, slip on my cute metallic pink Birkenstock sandals (a birthday gift from Winnie), snag my driver's license from my wallet, and head to the backyard with Sean's towel.

"It's your roomie!" I call as I approach the shower area. "I've got your towel and my ID, and I'm totally not looking." Boy, did I get an eyeful earlier. I had to stop in the yard and take a moment for a silent *wow*. He is hung, and it was pointing right at me. Because of me? Or because he's one of those guys who regularly jerks off in the shower? Hmm…he seems to find me irritating, so it was probably just his usual shower routine. I get it. Tension relief.

"Leave it on the bench," he growls. "Please," he adds belatedly.

I do; then I slap a hand over my eyes and hold up my driver's license in his direction. "I didn't realize you installed a shower out here. That's smart with the renovation."

"Could ya step away from the shower area?"

"Did you see my license?"

"Yeah, I saw it. Move it, please, away from the shower area."

I back away a few steps. He has an awesome Brooklyn accent I'm going to practice later. I have a knack for picking up regional accents after traveling most of my childhood with my opera singer mother. I never had roots or a true home, still don't. Sometimes I long for that stability. It's not easy to keep starting over in a new place, which is probably why I've learned to make myself at home wherever I land.

"More away," he demands.

It's a little late to be shy, but I respect his request and wander over to a border of deep purple tulips. I sense his glowering presence a few moments later and turn just as he stalks past me, heading for the house.

I catch up with him. "If you want the couch, I could take the air mattress."

He keeps walking, seeming to be in a hurry. I keep up. "If I wanted to sleep on the couch, I would have. It's mine. I made it."

"You made it? Wow! That's amazing. It's very comfortable." The couch is this deep blue cushy thing deep enough for two people to lounge on, almost like a full-size bed. It occurs to me he used to lounge on it with Winnie. Maybe he made it for her. "You're very talented."

He grunts in response like I'm irritating him again, but still holds the door for me, waiting for me to go inside ahead of him. Winnie was right—gentleman material.

"Thank you," I say as I brush by him. His piercing blue eyes meet mine briefly before he looks away, his dark scruffy jaw tight. He inclines his head the tiniest amount in acknowledgment of my thank you. Grumpy meets manners. He can't always be grumpy though, right? I'm sure we can get along if we just get back on the right foot.

He heads upstairs to get dressed, and I watch him go, admiring the hard planes of muscle on his broad shoulders and back. Definitely ideal security-guard material. No one would dare mess with him. How could Winnie leave out the bulging muscles? Yeah, I appreciate them. What woman wouldn't?

"I can feel your eyes boring into my back," he announces.

I flush and improvise away my obvious ogling. "Winnie said you're protective, so I was just wondering if you used to be a security guard."

"No." He stops short and turns. His shoulders draw back and his chest puffs out. "So she did talk about me."

"Only recently when she offered the couch." He deflates, so I quickly add, "She also said you were a gentleman."

He frowns. "Yeah, well, I'm thinking of hanging up that title." He turns and heads upstairs.

"Why?"

"Not working out for me," he grumbles.

I lean toward the stairwell where he just disappeared. "I think it's nice."

"Could ya *please* give me some privacy?" he barks.

Geez. Grump is out in full force. I can win him over. I'm a very likeable person. That's what my agent always says I have going for me. I win them over in the audition room just by being myself, even before I perform. It's why I keep booking pilots. This is my third one. The other two weren't picked up, but third time's the charm. Plus, I've done a perfume commercial and an educational series for school libraries. *Don't worry, Mom and Dad, that BFA in drama from NYU is totally paying off!* My student loans are killer, which is another reason I live as frugally as possible (besides not having a steady job). I'll get there. It's just a matter of the right project at the right time. Two years of auditioning and scraping by will all be like a distant dream once I get my big break. It only takes one.

I allow myself a small sigh before putting my license away and grabbing my shower stuff. That was good timing to find out about the shower. I moved in yesterday morning, so now that I don't have to make the daily trek to the gym for a shower, it frees up my schedule a bit. Not that it was overly full with the gym, improv class, and auditions. I'm not taking a waitressing job unless the pilot falls through, which it won't. *My time is now. I believe, I believe, I believe.*

Ooh, I know! I'll make Sean breakfast before he goes off to work. He's got the kind of job that requires lots of calories to sustain. Unlike the usual guys I meet, he gets those bulging muscles from actually using them, not from reps at a gym. I appreciate a hard worker since I am too, always hustling to make my career happen.

Once I'm under the shower spray, I'm surprised at how awesome it is. Good water pressure, warm, and it really is private out here with the wooden walls of the shower, the nearby rose trellises, and assorted plantings. I wonder if Sean was the one who turned my grandmother's modest garden into this paradise, and then my mind immediately shifts to Sean naked. I saw him in his full glory. Not that I'm interested. He acts like I'm a major inconvenience. Plus it's weird with him being Winnie's ex.

Winnie inherited our grandmother's townhouse because she was close to her. I was too young to get to know my grandmother that well, and my parents and I didn't visit her much because she was a little cool to my parents on account of my straitlaced dad (her son) disappointing her by marrying my artsy mother. My grandmother thought my mom's career took her away too much for her to be a good wife and mother, and they had a falling-out over it. But Dad and I traveled with Mom all over the world, and our little family was close. My parents live in Nashville now, which is cool, but not convenient for me to live there and still audition regularly. Mom's career wound down with age, as often happens with women's roles in the opera. Age prejudice sucks. She still has a beautiful voice. I can sing too, but my passion is the movies, which I hope one day to be in.

I skip washing my hair since I did it yesterday and go for the soap. I'm supposed to hear in the next two or three weeks about my pilot, and then I'm heading to LA. Grouchy Prince Sean is my temporary roomie. That's it. And it does give me peace of mind knowing there's a big strong guy around. It's not like that skeeze from LA is going to follow me here, but still. It doesn't hurt anyone for me to imagine Sean as my unofficial guard. I'll probably never have to call on him, but I could if I needed to, and that's the important part.

"Fantasy guard," I sing to myself as I wash. "How I welcome thee!" Threw a little Shakespeare style in there. I'm used to entertaining myself.

A few minutes later, I dry off and feel a little chilly. I rush inside, throw on some clothes—V-neck green T-shirt and black yoga pants—and head for the small kitchen. It's right next to the cozy den on the garden-level first floor, where I'm crashing on the couch. It's also the only floor with a functioning bathroom. What a nice place to land. I can hear Sean stomping around upstairs. Maybe he's getting some tools in place for his work here later. Winnie says he works nights and weekends on this place. I'm sure he'll appreciate a hearty breakfast before he goes to his day job.

I open the refrigerator and find only eggs, milk, and sliced stuff from the deli. I check the deli wrapper labels—ham and provolone. There's bread on the counter too. If only I was a genius chef and knew how to whip up something special from basic ingredients. Well, grilled cheese is carb and protein. That seems good for sustained energy. I'll add ham too. Hey, am I making a *croque monsieur*? I just might be. Lucky Sean to get a fancy hot breakfast before work. This will definitely get us back on track. I really can't take a tense home environment. I'm used to relaxed and easy.

I find a skillet in a cabinet and set it on the stove, turning on the gas flame. What else? Is there butter? I look around in case he leaves it out on the counter somewhere and then double-check the refrigerator, but there isn't any. I check the cabinets for oil or spray and come up short. Maybe the pan is already coated with some kind of nonstick stuff. No problem. I pull out a plate and assemble my very first *croque monsieur* (I think) and set it on the skillet.

I get us both glasses of water and set them on the beige laminate-topped island. I glance over at the *croque monsieur*, which still looks fine, so I set two napkins down, folded neatly on the diagonal. After his sandwich is done, I'll make one for me too.

I smell something burning and hurry over to flip the sandwich. Crap. Where's the spatula? I rifle through the drawers, wasting valuable flipping time, until I finally find it. I flip it over, and the now-melted cheese hits the skillet with a sharp sizzle. The bread is blackened, and smoke rises from the pan. I fan the smoke away. It's still salvageable. I can scrape off this black stuff and it'll taste great. I just need to wait a few minutes for this side to get nice and toasty. Damn, it's really smoky in here. I cough and open the back door in what was once a small dining room and is now empty space. I need a breeze. I open and close the door several times to air it out and, when that doesn't work, I rush to the window on the other side of the space in the den and open it.

Beep-beep-beep! Oh no! I set off the smoke detector. I turn off the stove and locate the smoke detector on the ceiling near the stairs. I can't quite reach to turn it off. It's not a fire just smoke! No need for alarm! I jump a few times in an attempt to push the button off and then go up a couple of steps and try to reach that way. No go. I fan the smoke away frantically with both hands.

"What the hell?" Sean barks from behind me.

I whirl and yell above the high-pitched beeping, "Can you turn it off? I can't reach. It's just smoke from burnt bread."

He reaches up and turns it off easily. He's probably six feet tall. "Great."

I relax as the beeping finally ceases. "I made you breakfast."

"Ya mean the burnt bread?"

"Just a little. I'll scrape off the burnt part."

He sits down on the steps and drops his head in his hands. His dark brown hair flops forward, still a little damp from the shower. He looks worn out and slightly despairing. I'm a careful observer of body language and expressions for my actor toolbox.

"I'll make you a fresh one," I offer in an upbeat tone. *Don't despair, roomie!*

He lifts his head. "The smoke detectors are the high-end kind from the home security company. They're wired to automatically call the fire department. Ya can't cancel the call once it goes out. I tried once before when Winnie burned dinner. They have to investigate and follow a routine inspection procedure."

"Winnie burned dinner? But she's a domestic goddess."

He gives me serious side-eye. "I distracted her."

I open my mouth and then shut it again. *Sex thing, got it.* Though it's hard to imagine my sweet, domestic goddess cousin with this rough-around-the-edges construction worker. I have so many questions.

He exhales sharply. "Now I'm gonna have to deal with them and wait for the all clear before I can get to work. Another delay. Just what I need."

"I'll take care of it. You go ahead to work."

"I work here," he says through his teeth.

"Oh, I thought you only worked here nights and weekends."

"I took the week off to make a dent in the renovation."

I glance toward the kitchen. "So, do you want to eat while we wait for the fire department?"

He lets out a breath and stalks over to the kitchen. I join him, and we both stare at the blackened sandwich with brown curdled cheese and ham glued to the skillet.

"I'm sure it still tastes good," I say. "It's a *croque monsieur.*" My French accent is spot on. Mom's job took us to Paris many times.

He gives me a skeptical look, his brows lifting. "Then you eat it."

I grab the spatula and work to get the sandwich off the skillet, jabbing it from several directions before it finally comes off mostly intact. I set it on the plate I left on the counter, grab a knife, and scrape it down to the nonburnt part of the bread. I can sense his judgey eyes on me, but I ignore that because I'm determined to make my kind breakfast gesture the cornerstone of our friendly living arrangement. Once he sees proof that my cooking is adequate, he'll eat this kind gesture up.

I smile at him before taking a big bite of sandwich. *Gross.* "Delicious," I lie, holding it in the corner of my mouth. It tastes like smoke and something both funky and slippery.

He laughs. "The ham and cheese are ancient."

I grab a napkin and spit it out. "Why didn't you tell me?"

"More fun this way." He glances over at the island, where I've set our glasses of water and napkins. "You don't hafta cook for me."

"I know." I toss the sandwich in the garbage and grab the old ham and cheese and toss those too. I turn to him. "I was trying to get us on the right footing. I want us to get along."

He arches a brow and takes a drink from the glass of water I poured him. "Great water."

I laugh a little. "Sorry I delayed your work. I could help you."

"No!" He crosses his fingers like he's warding me off. "You stay in your corner and I'll stay in mine."

"That sounds like we're boxers in the ring. I don't want to fight."

"You stay in your corner, and we won't."

I step closer. "But it'll be tense. I prefer a relaxed environment."

He steps back, pivots, and goes to the cabinet, pulling out a protein bar and ripping the plastic wrapper off. He takes a bite and speaks around it. "This is breakfast."

My stomach growls. I'm not going to beg him for breakfast. I'll go to the market and get some essentials later. Yesterday I had leftovers from Winnie.

"And coffee," he says, getting the coffee maker going.

I watch him work on his simple breakfast, tension apparent in every movement. "Are you always this tense?"

He doesn't bother to turn around. "You'd be tense too if you had a tight deadline on a job you really cared about doing right, all while working a day job."

"I'm good at massage," I say, lifting my hands and flexing them. "My friends say I have healing hands. I was thinking of picking that up as a side gig while I wait for my big break." And I suck at waitressing.

He slants a glance at me over his shoulder. "No, thanks." He presses a button on the coffee maker, turns and leans against the counter, grabbing the protein bar and finishing it in a few bites. "Don't cook. Just use the microwave or get takeout. I'm taking the kitchen down to the studs soon anyway, so you might as well get used to making do." He shoves a hand through his hair, rumpling it. "You're not gonna be able to sleep down here while I'm working on this level. There'll be too much dust. I don't know what to do with you." He exhales sharply and gives me a hard look. "You'll have to sleep on the floor in one of the upstairs bedrooms. I'm not exactly set here for guests. Couldn't ya just deal with the crappy love situation at Winnie's place?"

I press my lips together, trying to decide how much to reveal about my dislike of Colin. Then I just decide to lay it out there. "Please don't share this with Winnie, but I don't like Colin. He's very rigid, not tense like you are right now. I mean, like, he has a permanent stick up his ass."

He snorts.

"And his dark eyes are cold and calculating, like a shark. I mentioned it once to Winnie, but she said he's just really smart, so that's what that look is about. So, you know, whatever, I don't have to marry the guy, but I don't want to live in close quarters with him. He gives me the creeps."

"You'd rather live in close quarters with me, a total stranger?"

"I'd rather live with a protective gentleman with piercing blue eyes. Those eyes are direct and straightforward."

His jaw drops before he snaps it shut. He smirks just a tiny bit as he studies me with his piercing blue eyes, probably glad I find him preferable to Colin, since my cousin obviously didn't. Then he rubs the back of his neck and blows out a breath. He's resigned to his roomie fate, but still tense.

I can't help but think I had a teensy bit to do with that tension, surprising him as his new roommate, even though Winnie said he was already grumpy about the renovation. She didn't give him advance notice about me because she was tired of dealing with his snarling. I assured her I'd win him over, and I will.

"Let's start over. Hi! I'm Josie." I offer my hand just as sirens roar down the street.

He looks to the ceiling. "I know. Believe me, I know."

He shakes his head and heads out the front door to meet the fire trucks.

While he's busy outside talking to the firefighters, I notice the coffee is ready. I find a mug and grab the handle of the glass pot to pour him a cup, when the pot handle slips from my fingers. Shit! It bounces off the counter and drops to the hard ceramic-tiled floor, where it shatters, coffee splashing everywhere. I jump back and quickly run my arm under cold water where the hot coffee splashed. This is why my waitressing tips suck. I don't know what it is about me and kitchens, but we don't get along. That's what happens when you never have a true home. I can only do the basics in the kitchen and not all that well. I only attempted breakfast because I thought he was heading out to his day job soon, and I didn't want to miss the chance to do something nice for him.

I hear Sean and the firefighters step inside, and look over my shoulder. "Careful! There's broken glass and coffee on the floor. Small accident. I'll get it cleaned up in a minute."

Sean frowns and strides toward me. I brace myself for more of his grumbling, or maybe he'll yell at me, telling me to leave and never come back.

Instead he leans close, staring at the red splotches on my forearm under the running water of the faucet. "You burned yourself."

"It's nothing. First degree, and I got it cooled right away."

He meets my eyes up close and, for the first time, his eyes are less piercing and more concerned. His voice is gruffly tender. "Ya really wanna help, don't ya?"

My pulse skitters. "Yeah. I was trying to. I guess I should've found another way, outside the kitchen." I turn off the water, and he hands me a paper towel.

The firefighters are inspecting the area around us, but all of my focus is on him as he lifts my arm in a light hold, checking it at different angles.

"It's okay," I say softly. "I'll clean up."

He frowns. "You're barefoot."

"I'm wearing sandals." I gasp as he lifts me by the waist and sets me on top of the island.

"I'll do it. Don't move."

I watch him clean up at my feet, occasionally rising to address the firefighters, who are now checking every room in the place. I caused this disaster he's fixing. And he didn't come in here like a boxer coming out of his corner to knock me out either. He did it kinda tenderly. With care.

I can see why Winnie dated him now. He's got some tenderness hiding underneath the gruffness. I smile to myself. This roomie situation can totally work.

He's complex, and I like that as an actor. I'm going to consider this an acting intensive and study him for the character of uber-skilled construction worker with a heart of gold. Maybe I'm embellishing a bit with the heart of gold, but I have good instincts for people, and my instincts tell me he's a good guy.

Now I just have to make myself indispensable.

3

———

Sean

I see the firefighters out and stand on the sidewalk for a minute, watching as they return to their trucks. I'm an hour delayed with work on the upstairs bathroom, and it's all Josie's fault. I thought she'd be a distraction just by being her too-beautiful cheery self, but it's much worse than that. She's a walking disaster. The more she tries to "help," the more work I'll have to do. I need her to leave.

I go back inside and find her in the kitchen with her back to me.

"Josie."

She whirls and quickly chews and swallows, looking guilty. "Sorry. I took one of your protein bars. I'll get you more."

My irritation fades. She was hungry. Who knows when her last meal was? She's a poor out-of-work actress. Yet she still tried to cook me breakfast before getting herself something.

"Don't worry about it," I say. "I'm used to sharing my food. I grew up with five brothers who eat like it's an Olympic sport."

"Thanks. I was too hungry to wait." She takes another bite, blissing out on protein bar like she's starving and it's a real treat. It's bland at best. She quickly finishes the protein bar and says, "Let me be useful to you."

"What's your schedule look like?" I'm hoping she's got something going on. I need stretches of work time to focus, where I don't have to worry about what she's messing up.

"I do yoga first thing in the morning, gym workout in the late afternoon for a pick-me-up, and I have improv class Thursday night in the city at seven. Other than that, it's wait for my agent to check in with an audition I might be right for." She lifts her arms. "I'm all yours for however long you need me."

My gaze drops to her exposed stomach with outlined muscle along her abs. Workouts are paying off. I jerk my head up.

She drops her arms and smiles brightly. "I'm sure working on a renovation will be even more of a workout than the gym."

I don't have the heart to kick out a starving out-of-work actress. Not that I easily could, since I don't own the place. I stifle a sigh. It's only for a couple of weeks, right? Then she'll go out to LA. And I'm only here for a week full-time before I go back to my day job. Then I'll be too busy to even notice her. I can put up with her for a week. I'll just give her something to do separate from me. Only what can she do that won't mess up anything?

"Ever use tools?" I ask.

"No. But I'm a quick study. I'll watch you, and I'm sure I'll pick it right up. I'll be like your apprentice."

I frown. No way I can have her watching me work all day in the close quarters of the third-floor bathroom. Finally, I think of something. "You can wipe down the tile in the fourth-floor bathroom. There's a layer of dust and smudged grout. You need to wipe down the tile in the shower and then the floor tile. Think you can do that?"

She grins. "Sure can, boss man."

I find myself smiling and turn away. I don't want to be too friendly. "I'll get you a sponge and a scrub brush." I head upstairs, where I stashed my tools and supplies in an empty bedroom.

She follows on my heels. "How far along is the bathroom I'm working on?"

"Just waiting on the countertops to be cut at the tile shop. They have the sinks to custom cut the counters to fit. Should be in by next Friday; then I'll hook it up with the faucets."

"Cool. And I assume the toilet and shower work."

"Yeah, but I haven't been using them since I don't want to risk getting the vanity wet before the counter is installed."

"Then why am I wiping everything down? Won't that get the vanity wet too?"

"Not if you're careful. It's just a damp sponge." I halt on the third-floor landing and turn back to her. Maybe this was a bad idea. Her kitchen history makes her seem clumsy.

She holds up a finger. "I can see you're having second thoughts, but I swear I'm only a disaster in the kitchen. You didn't have a problem when I was in the powder room, right?"

I consider this. Besides the fact that she was in the powder room when she shouldn't have been here at all, she did leave it in one piece.

She gestures for me to back up, and joins me on the landing. "Would I risk getting off on the wrong foot again? No, I would not. We're a team from here on out. I'm going to carefully wipe everything down without getting the vanity wet, and you're going to love the results. You'll say, Josie, you should be the sparkle shiner on all my jobs. We'll always get top dollar!"

I'm smiling again. "Sparkle shiner?"

She grins. "For sure."

I shake my head and head for the bedroom with cleaning supplies, grabbing the sponge, scrubber, and bucket. I hand them to her. "Use the tub spout to fill the bucket with a small amount of water for rinsing the sponge and scrubber. If ya have any problem, stop whatever you're doing and come get me. I'll be tiling the shower in the bathroom on this floor." I point down the hall. "It's in the corner there, right under the bathroom you'll be in."

She brightens. "That's convenient. We'll be able to hear each other working, so it's like we're keeping each other company."

I keep my expression neutral. "That's generally how bathrooms work since that's where the plumbing runs. Not to keep each other company."

Her face falls. "Right."

A stab of guilt hits. I hurt her feelings. She so wants to be my friendly roomie. I shake it off. I really need to focus. She's a distraction mostly because I haven't been with a woman in so long. If it were one of my brothers working upstairs, I wouldn't give them a second thought. I'll work on getting with a woman—a different woman—once I finally finish this renovation. I restrain myself from making amends with her and head to the bathroom to get to work.

A short while later, I hear her coming down the stairs. *Please tell me she didn't screw something up already.* I poke my head out. "Everything okay?"

She smiles, her blue eyes sparkling. Her hair is back up in a messy knot, her neck exposed, a soft curve to her shoulder. I force my gaze back to her eyes. "No problem, boss man. Just want to get something. Don't let me distract you."

"Too late," I mutter under my breath after she leaves. I smooth compound on the drywall. I'm three rows in on a staggered brick pattern for the white tile in the shower and working my way up. I turn on my work music, hoping to tune out whatever she's doing and focus. I've got a small speaker set up in here.

Fortunately, the music does the trick, and I get into a steady flow, tiling and occasionally pausing to head to the bedroom, where I left my tile saw, and cutting a tile to fit at the edge of a row. I'm making great progress and liking the results. And then I hear the water turn on above me, and it sounds like a full-on shower. No. I'm not going up there. She's probably rinsing down the shower walls. No need to panic.

I turn off the music and listen. She's singing a show tune. She sounds really good, actually.

I go back to work. Several minutes later, the shower is still running. Shouldn't the walls be rinsed by now? I purposely don't use that shower so I don't risk getting water on the nearby exposed wood vanity, which is still missing the countertop. She'd better have the glass shower door completely closed.

I blow out a breath. Better check.

There's no door on either bathroom because I needed the extra doorway space to fit stuff in, which means when I arrive in the doorway of the fourth-floor bathroom, I have a clear view of Josie naked in the shower, singing as she flings water at the tile with her fingers in what looks like a jazzy dance routine.

She's graceful, lithe, her sweet curves slick with water. Pink nipples on full breasts, smooth toned stomach, flare of hips, curve of her ass, shapely legs. I take it all in, my gut tightening, the blood rushing through my veins. I need to leave, but I can't seem to move. Fuck. It's been way too long for me.

She turns slightly, and I back up quickly.

I'm stealthy as a cat making my way back downstairs. She can do whatever weird naked cleaning dance she wants to, and I'm not going to say boo about it. The glass door was completely closed at least. I'll fix whatever mess she makes getting out of there afterward, when I'm sure she's dressed. This is basic survival.

She keeps singing.

I go back to work, but I'm overheated and can't focus. Sweet slick curves are imprinted on my brain. Dammit.

I head downstairs and go out to the backyard for some fresh air, following the path along the garden. This space always calms me. Okay, it's not that bad. Yes, I saw her naked, but she doesn't know I saw her naked. This doesn't have to be weird. Then I remember she saw me naked in the outdoor shower, and I definitely did know it. Great! We're even. Naked happened, and now it's over.

My phone vibrates in my jeans pocket and I check it. Winnie. I texted her earlier to call me. I punch the button and she speaks right away in a rush of words.

"Hi, I guess you met Josie by now. I hope you're not being grumpy to her."

So she didn't forget to tell me about her cousin. She chose not to for some reason, just like I was beginning to suspect. "Ya could've given me a heads-up."

"You would've raised a fuss, and I'm tired of your complaining. It's my place, and Josie needed a place to crash. I told her you were a gentleman and she could feel safe there."

I clench my jaw. She acts like I'm a monk. Like Josie never had to consider I might put the moves on her. And here I suspected Winnie sent Josie here to distract me so I'd fail at my deadline and she could replace me with another contractor. Obviously, they both thought this would just be a neutral roommate situation. Any red-blooded man would want Josie!

Winnie goes on. "She had a scare with an aggressive man in LA, and I knew you just being you would reassure her."

My brows draw down. What? Then I remember Josie asked me if I'd ever been a security guard. "What happened?"

"He got aggressive after she said no, and she ran and called nine-one-one. She managed to stay safe, but it scared her. I offered to let her stay with me, but she didn't want to intrude on me and Colin. We only have a one-bedroom. Our grandmother's place has plenty of room."

I shove a hand through my hair. Josie was chased by an aggressor who wouldn't take no for an answer? And here I've been growling at her nonstop. Not that she seemed intimidated by that. She has zero street smarts. All that open eagerness, her expression showing every thought and emotion, her sexy naked body. *Don't think about it. Never happened.*

I scowl. "She's a distraction. She's definitely gonna slow me down, and I've got no place to put her once I start on the kitchen. She can't live in a demo zone."

"You're living in a demo zone just fine. You're just using

her as an excuse not to finish the job. We need it on the market June first. Colin wants to buy us a co-op on the Upper East Side, and there's an opening in a very prestigious building. We're going for an interview with the co-op board tonight."

Her snippy tone sets me on edge, and I bite back a curse. Looks like Mr. Moneybags strikes again. I can't let my irritation with Winnie put me on the outs with her. I want to keep this job and finish it to my standards. This project has been mine for more than a year. It's a personal challenge, a rare historic gem that I will restore, all me. And it won't hurt to have it in the Rourke Management portfolio either. My family business is branching out from construction to real estate development, and this place is a prime example of the value of renovating.

"Please, Sean. Just make it happen. I trust you to do the job right. That's the only reason I've let this project go on as long as it has, but it needs to get done."

"I know," I say through my teeth. "I took the week off work to make progress here." And you threw a sexy wrench in the works with your cousin.

"Great! I really appreciate it. Now get back to work! Ha-ha. Bye!"

I punch the button to end the call and march upstairs, determined to make progress. I start tiling and notice the shower's off above me. Josie's singing again, but I can't make out the tune. She's probably on all fours, wiping down the floor tile. Hopefully dressed. Of course she's dressed! I blast my music, tuning her out.

I'm startled later by a tap on my shoulder. I turn, irritated by the interruption, but then Josie beams her sunshine smile at me. I can't growl at the woman who showed up here looking for safe harbor after some aggressive asshole went after her. Especially knowing Winnie's fiancé gives her the creeps. I'm all Josie has, and I hate the fact that someone as open and friendly as she is ever felt threatened.

"Finished!" she exclaims. "Do you want to come up and see? I think you'll like the sparkly results."

"I'm sure it's fine." I'll play guard, keeping watch with my hands to myself. Probably more than normal. I stifle a groan. This is going to be torture.

She steps closer. Tendrils of red hair escaped the knot on top, still damp from her shower dance of cleaning. Naked Josie flashes through my mind, and I focus on her toes peeking out of sandals. Even her toes are cute.

"It's great," she says. "Except for the missing sinks, faucets, and counter. Are you sure you don't want to check my work, boss man?"

"I'll take your word for it."

She gestures for me to join her. "Come see."

"Busy." I go back to tiling. Josie is off-limits. She wants a guard and that's all I'll be.

"What's your number? I'll take a few photos and text you. It'll only take a sec to see."

She's so persistent it's hard not to growl. I turn to her, and she looks back at me expectantly. I guess that's the kind of persistence you need to keep auditioning in the face of rejection after rejection. I give her my number, even though it feels like another step closer. She'll probably text me regularly now, and then I'll have to answer so she doesn't feel like we're not friendly roommates. And I didn't even want a roommate in the first place! And I definitely didn't want a beautiful sexy naked woman as a *friend*.

Not naked. Stop. She's fully dressed, adding me to her phone contacts, but I can see her body in my mind. Even fully dressed she's a sight. Her full breasts under her green T-shirt with its peekaboo hem that keeps giving me glimpses of her abs. The black yoga pants hugging her curvy hips and toned legs.

She turns and heads upstairs. Sweet curve of her ass.

Dammit.

4

Josie

I do believe I've proved my worth as a renovation helper. Whatever Sean's working on, I'm right there to hand him a tool, a tile, or a drink of water. I tried adding compound to the tile ahead of time for him to set it in place, but that didn't go over well *at all*. Apparently, the compound goes on the wall, not the tile, and only *he* can touch that stuff. In any case, I've made a thorough study of him at work. Who knows, maybe I'll play a construction worker one day in a movie.

We're in the third-floor bathroom, as usual. Actually, I'm standing outside it on his orders while he does the floor. Okay, I may have exaggerated a teensy bit on Sean accepting me as his helper. I get the feeling he barely tolerates me sometimes, even though I've made myself indispensable all week. Like right now, I have a glass of water for him in one hand and a handful of plastic spacers in the other, which I hand him when he needs one. On top of my usefulness in the renovation, I set a place for dinner for him every night and serve up the takeout I order for us, so he can sit down to a nice dinner with me. We eat at the kitchen island, sitting on two wooden stools. I clean up afterward too. Anything to lighten his load.

It's now Thursday and, despite all the great progress

we've made in this bathroom, he's even more grumpy and tense than ever. He only answers my attempts at conversation with a single curt word. Sometimes just a monosyllable. It almost takes away from his sweaty muscled gorgeousness. Almost.

I watch as he carries a large tile to the edge of the room. He oozes raw masculine power in his sweat-dampened black T-shirt, jeans, and work boots. His dark brown hair is sexily tousled from where he shoved his hand through it. And he has the most gorgeous piercing blue eyes, scruffy square jaw, and strong corded neck. I've studied his neck from all angles, and there's something so masculine and sexy about it. So, yeah, I've done my fair share of ogling in the name of unrequited lust. It's kinda fun when I don't have to worry he'll reciprocate. If he was actually interested in me, he'd at least smile once in a while. Besides, Winnie would *not* appreciate me going for her ex. It's, like, there's a million guys in the world and you have to choose my ex? Awkward, tense, maybe a little jealousy stabbing through. I've imagined the whole scenario and concluded, all things considered, he's my fantasy man.

"How did you and Winnie meet?" I ask.

"Fundraiser." *Single curt word.*

Still, I'm intrigued. "Let me guess, she won you in a bachelor auction and brought you home."

His brows lift, but he keeps his eyes on his work. "No." *Monosyllable.*

"C'mon, that's a great how-we-met story."

He keeps tiling.

Not even a monosyllable this time, and I'm dying to know. "Okay, I'll bite. What was the fundraiser for? How did you connect?"

He doesn't bother to look up. "Why does it matter?"

"I'm curious. You just seem like an unusual pairing. She's so cultured and sophisticated—"

"And I'm not," he says flatly.

"You're grounded and practical."

He doesn't disagree, just walks out to get another large

tile. The moment he gets back, I follow up. "Was it a fundraiser for the art gallery?"

He heaves a manly sigh. "It was a fundraiser for Habitat for Humanity. I've been helping them build houses for years, and the director asked if I could help with fundraising. So I did. I met her at a restaurant fundraiser here in Park Slope."

"What's a restaurant fundraiser?"

"The restaurant owner agrees to host a dinner on what's normally a slow night. I draw in customers, and a portion of the night's profits go to Habitat for Humanity. It works really well. People like to get out for a good cause, and the restaurant owner appreciates a full house on a slow night. It's good for follow-on business for the restaurant too. I've done a bunch of them."

"So Winnie was in the neighborhood and decided to show up?"

He starts tiling again. "Yup."

I smile a little, imagining how it went down. "You were probably dressed up, smiling your most charming smile, wowing her with your gentleman manners, and she was overcome."

He barks out a laugh. *Score!* My first laugh from him. His blue eyes sparkle as he lifts his head. "Ya nailed it. She said I was a charming gentleman. Maybe I liked playing the part."

"But it's not who you are, deep down, which is ultimately why you broke up."

He stops smiling. "We broke up because she walked out the door to live with another guy."

I suck in air. "She cheated on you."

His expression closes, his voice even. "She said it was an affair of the heart, not the body."

"Same difference! Oh, Sean, I'm so sorry. That's awful."

He goes back to work. "I don't wanna talk about her."

I'm actually really surprised Winnie would do that. She's a genuinely sweet person. Colin must've swept her off her feet. Love works in mysterious ways, I guess. Hasn't happened for me yet, but I'm young, so there's plenty of time. Plus, I was born on Valentine's Day, which means I was made for something dazzlingly romantic one day. Pretty sure.

I take in the tense set of his jaw. Now I feel bad for bringing up a sore subject with Winnie. I keep quiet, watching him work. It's pretty amazing the way he perfectly places everything. It would be easy to make a mess of it. He has to cut a lot of tile just right to fit this space.

I cheer when he sets the last corner tile. "Ta-dah! Floor is done!"

He looks over his shoulder at me from the floor. "No." *Crap. Back to monosyllables.*

"What do you still have to do?"

He gets to his feet. "Grout." *Another monosyllable.*

"Then what?" *There's no way he can answer that in a mono-syllable.*

He plants his hands on his hips, arching his back. "Do I really need to run the schedule by ya?"

My skill at drawing out more words is slightly dampened by his grouchiness.

"I'm your renovation helper."

He looks skeptical like he always does when I say that.

"And I'm looking at this as an acting intensive for the character of uber-skilled construction worker."

He turns away to open the window, but not before I catch the tiniest lift of his lips. He likes that I complimented him. I always zero in on micro-expressions, the tiniest change that could indicate an emotion. All part of my acting toolbox. The close-up captures just those kinds of nuanced expressions.

"Well?" I ask in a teasing voice. "What's next, boss man?" I noticed he talks more when I call him that.

He exhales sharply. "After the grout dries, I paint the walls, and then I put in the toilet, vanities, lighting fixtures, and towel bars. Then I arrange for the counters to be installed. Two separate vanities in this one."

"Fantastic! So when do we demo the kitchen?"

He scowls. "*We* don't demo. *We* don't do anything. *I* demo this weekend."

"I can swing a hammer. I saw regular people do it on one of those home renovation shows."

"Don't ya have anything better to do than shadow me?" he barks.

I stiffen because he hasn't barked at me like that since I first surprised him by moving in. He's been very even-toned, though monosyllabic for the most part. "You know, if I were working on a tight deadline to renovate a house, I'd want all hands on deck. I'm free labor and all you do is grump at me."

"*I'm* the free labor. *You're* the uninvited couch crasher."

"I *was* invited." I set the spacers and glass of water down in the hallway and walk away. If he's going to be so ungrateful, then he can forget having me as his renovation helper and all-around useful, friendly roomie. We'll be like two ships never passing in the night.

"Josie."

I whirl. He's standing in the hallway. Not friendly looking, exactly, but definitely not scowling. Maybe he'll even apologize for barking at me. "Yes?"

"I'm demo'ing the kitchen Saturday morning. Pick a room on the top floor to sleep in tomorrow night."

His tone is even, like we're back to being roomies, not irritating people stuck with each other, which is exactly how I'm starting to feel. He's the irritating one. I've never been more helpful in my life.

I salute him jauntily. I don't want to fight with my irritating roomie/fantasy man/unofficial guard. "Serve up your own dinner tonight. I'm going to the city for my improv class."

His brows lift. "What time will ya be back?"

"Why? Do I have a curfew?"

"I just don't wanna be surprised by a bump in the night."

"Relax. Class ends at eight thirty. I won't be back that late."

I head toward the stairs.

His deep voice sounds close behind me, startling me. The man moves like a ninja. "Text me if you want me to meet you at the subway stop and walk you home."

I turn, surprised at the kind offer. "Thanks, but it's only a few blocks. I've got the fast New Yorker stride down."

"Where're ya from?"

It's the first personal question he's asked since we met four days ago. Maybe he's warming up to me. "I grew up all over the world, traveling with my mom's career. She's an opera singer. But I went to NYU for college, so I'm used to the mean city streets." I laugh.

He mutters, "Later," before heading back to work.

Guess he didn't warm up that much, but I do appreciate his concern for my safety. He really is an excellent unofficial guard. I've slept soundly ever since I got here. There's something so nice about knowing his big muscled body is right upstairs. For safety reasons.

And a few fantasies.

~

Sean

I'm strangely out of sorts, and I don't know why. I finished the grout in time to call it quits for a late dinner, so I'm right on the schedule I assigned myself. I should be feeling good, eating leftover Thai food at the kitchen island, and watching the Yankees on my laptop. I've accomplished a lot under extremely difficult circumstances. It's not easy to focus on work while Josie hovers nearby, all sexy good cheer. I scrub a hand over my face. Hell. Do I actually miss her? She's joined me for dinner every night this week right here at this island, sharing about auditions and all the different kinds of acting classes she's been to. I didn't have anything to add, it's all new to me, but that never seems to bother her. She smiles at me a lot. It makes her blue eyes sparkle, her cheeks pinken, a warm energy radiating out from her, brightening the whole day.

What is wrong with me? I finally get a break from her, and I'm sitting here imagining her smile.

I shake my head at myself and finish up dinner, banishing thoughts of Josie from my mind. After I clear my dish and toss the take-out box, I head to the couch I haven't gotten to relax on since she moved in. This is my spot. Her pink fleece blanket and pillow are neatly folded on one end. I take a seat on the opposite end and stretch out to watch the game on my laptop.

Time passes slowly, and I realize I'm listening for her. It's nine fifteen. She said her class ended at eight thirty, so she should be back around nine thirty or ten, depending where her class is in the city. We're only forty minutes from midtown here.

The Yankees win in extra innings, and she's still not home. It's ten thirty. I check my phone. No text from her. She doesn't text me a lot since she's always in my face, but every night she texts me that dinner is ready. It's weirdly domestic, considering she doesn't cook. All she does is set the takeout on plates for us. It's really not a big deal.

Where is she? Should I text her?

The last thing I want is to look like I'm worried about her. She said she's used to the city. Surely she can find her way back to Brooklyn safely. She doesn't need me going overprotective guard dog on her. That's the only reason I let her hang around when I work, even though she's a huge distraction. She just seems more relaxed when she's near me, and I think it's because she feels safe.

I set the laptop aside and head out the front door, looking down the street for her. Nothing. Should I take a walk to the subway stop?

Okay, I'm taking a short walk. It doesn't mean I'm worried. I'm allowed to take a walk if I feel like it. Lots of people walking around here. I keep checking, but none of them are the red-haired beauty I usually ignore.

I go back home after my walk to the subway and settle back on the couch, only this time I can't relax. It's well past ten thirty. She should've been home by now. I'm going to text her. I set the laptop aside and pull out my phone. Hold up. Do I really want to cross this line? She'll think I actually thought about her when she wasn't here. That implies something more than just roommates. Women always read into these things.

I glance at the door. Fuck it.

Thought you'd be home by now. Where are you? I delete that. Too worried sounding.

Where's your improv class? Delete. Stalkerish.

Hey, did the subway break down? My finger hovers over the send button. Casual enough? The door opens, and I immediately delete the text.

She steps inside, her color high. She's in a frilly light purple blouse, tight jeans, and black heels. Her red hair is down, smooth with a slight wave, pink lips, tiny silver hoop earrings, and her blue eyes are lined with dark color that gives them a dramatic striking look. I see her so much in just a casual T-shirt and yoga pants with no makeup I can't help but notice every detail. She's casually glamorous, a future movie star that I can't stop thinking about. "Hello, boss man!"

I fucking love it when she calls me that. I don't know why. Maybe being second born, being passed over for CEO in favor of my older brother, I was never top dog. And every instinct in me wants to be. *Be cool. Distance.* "You're late."

She sets my laptop on the deep bay window ledge behind the couch and flops down next to me. "We went out for drinks after. Class was so fun. How was your night?"

I sound like an overprotective ass, but I can't seem to help myself. "I'm tired, and I wanted to go to bed, but I couldn't relax when you were so much later than you said you'd be."

Her eyes widen. "You are *really* harshing my martini mellow. What gives?"

"You said class ends at eight thirty. I thought you'd be home an hour ago."

She leans her shoulder against me. "Aww, did my guard dog worry?"

"Hell yes, I worried. You have no street smarts, just smiling, open and friendly with everyone, making your way home alone late at night."

She smiles up at me in her warm sunshiny way, her blue eyes dancing with good humor. "Ridiculous. I think you can go ahead and admit it now. I grew on you. You actually care about me."

I look straight ahead. "I don't—look, I was just concerned."

She squeezes my arm, and it warms at her touch. She smells sweet like fruity flowers. "Because I grew on you. I'm not so bad to have around. Right, roomie?"

I stand abruptly, realizing my mistake in waiting up for her. I need distance and fast. She's entirely too appealing in her relaxed martini state. "Next time text if you're gonna be later than you said you were."

I stalk off toward the stairs.

"Sean?"

I stop, but I don't turn around. "What?" I growl in my fiercest tone.

Silence.

I turn around to see if I hurt her feelings with my harsh tone. I just desperately need distance.

She gives me a sly look. "You should go to improv class with me next time. I think it'll help you relax."

"I don't have time for improv class."

She stands and slowly walks toward me, her hips swaying. My senses go on high alert. Her voice is a throaty purr. "It'll make you worry less if you can walk me home though, wouldn't it?"

I swallow hard. "I wasn't really worried. I was concerned. There's a difference."

She closes the distance and smiles up at me. "Would it kill you to admit I grew on you?"

Yes. Because that is one step too close for comfort. "I just want ya to be safe. Winnie told me about that guy in LA."

She frowns. "Yeah."

"I won't let anyone bother you. You're safe here. Just keep me in the loop so I know when to be concerned."

She bites her lower lip, and my gut tightens. "Can I tell you a secret?"

I hesitate because that feels too intimate, but she goes on anyway.

"Ever since I moved in with you, I haven't had a single nightmare about that horrible man. I've felt at peace, so thank you."

"Uh, you're wel..." I trail off in surprise. Her arms are wrapped around my middle in a tight hug. Her cheek presses against my chest and, when I glance down, she's smiling. Ah, hell.

I wrap my arms around her and let out a breath that almost feels like relief. She's here, she's safe, and she feels surprisingly good in my arms. Relief slowly shifts to awareness of her warm body pressed against mine. I've kept her at arm's length all week, and now she's awakening desire I've ruthlessly pushed down with every ounce of willpower I possess. I don't know how much willpower reserves I have left.

Her head lifts, her eyes soft. "I'm glad you're my unofficial guard and roommate."

Do not kiss her. "How much did you have to drink tonight?"

"One martini. Just enough to give me a nice buzz."

One martini is nothing.

She sighs and traces her finger over one of my biceps, staring at it. "I'm a bit of a lightweight."

Do not kiss the drunk girl. "Not much of a drinker, huh?"

"Nope. You?"

"Just a beer now and then."

"Mmm-hmm." Both her hands cup the sides of my neck and slide down my shoulders. "You're so nicely muscled, and I'm extremely fond of your neck. It's thick and corded."

Haven't heard that before. "Thanks." I drop my hands from her and take a step back. "Goodnight."

"Wait!"

I do, even though there's a playful sparkle to her eyes that makes me wary.

She takes a step closer and looks up at me from under her lashes. I'm in dangerous territory, but I can't seem to move away. "In improv, one person suggests something and then the other has to say 'yes, and,' and play along. You want to try it with me?"

My voice comes out hoarse. "I'm not an actor."

"Just try it. You say, 'close your eyes, Josie.'"

"Close your eyes, Josie."

She closes them, lifting her face to mine. "Yes, and kiss me."

I'm tempted, so tempted.

Her eyes open, locking on mine for an intense moment. Then her hand slides to the nape of my neck, her fingers in my hair, and she tugs me down to her, her eyes drifting closed. I don't resist. Curiosity? Loneliness? Plain old lust? I don't know, and I don't care. My lips meet hers in a soft kiss that only makes me crave more. I can't give in to this need. She's my ex's cousin, and she's out of here the first chance she gets.

I pull away, but she grabs my head and pulls me back in for another kiss. Raw desire floods my veins. I deepen the kiss, and then at the first tentative touch of her tongue on mine, I lose the iron grip of control, diving in hungrily. My hand tangles in her hair, the other cupping her ass and pressing her against me. Need like I've never felt before overwhelms my good sense. She returns the kiss passionately, and I'm lost in her sweet heat.

She breaks the kiss. "We shouldn't do this. You're my cousin's ex. It's weird."

"You're leaving when you get your pilot."

She beams a smile at me. "You really believe I'll get it?"

"It's easier to think that."

"Why?"

I open my mouth and shut it. Why don't I want to get closer? Fuck Winnie. She left me. What if Josie did stick around?

I'm not up to a relationship. That's the problem. But I've been avoiding a hookup with her too. Something about Josie feels dangerous, like I could fall hard and never recover. That's all the reason I need to keep my distance. I don't want to get burned again.

"Goodnight, roomie," I say, dropping my hands from her and heading upstairs.

"Goodnight, boss man!" she calls.

A reluctant smile tugs at my lips. Maybe I do want to be the boss. For the first time I wonder if I should branch out with my own business. I shake my head. Look at how optimistic Josie infected my brain. Like I could ever step away from my family's business. I'm rooted here in Brooklyn with my family and our business. Josie will go wherever the job is. I did the right thing stepping away. There's no future for us, and some part of me knows a casual fling wouldn't end up being that way for me. I already care about her too much.

$$5$$

Sean

I check in at my real job the next morning. It's Friday, and our CEO, my older brother, Dylan, is back early from his honeymoon in Italy with his wife, Ariana. Their plan to cruise the Italian coast was thwarted by a serious storm that looked like it would be sticking around for several days. Dylan is actually whistling as he walks into our construction office. Guess married life agrees with him. I know Ariana well. She was in my grade at school and lived next door to us growing up. She was always a quiet shy girl, which is probably why I was never interested in her. I like someone with more fire in her, more energy, an open friendliness that says she's up for anything. I am *not* describing Josie. I'm speaking in general terms about what I normally go for when I have the time and energy for a woman in my life. Which is not now.

"Hey," Dylan says, giving me a slap on the back. "Ready to get back to real work?"

"Yeah, almost. I'll be back here full-time on Monday. Just checking in today."

He smiles, his blue eyes sparkling, all tanned and relaxed. I can't remember the last time *I* felt relaxed. "How's it going? You gonna wrap up at Winnie's place soon?"

"Getting there. I'm finishing up the bathroom; then I need

to get the kitchen done, and a few tweaks here and there before inspections."

He nods and heads to the makeshift kitchen setup on a table in the corner of the office, whistling again.

"How was Italy?"

"Fantastic!"

I join him as he helps himself to coffee. "You're awfully happy to be back at work. Aren't ya upset your vacation was cut short?"

"Nah. We still had five days to see everything we wanted to see in Rome and Venice. We'll go back for an anniversary to check out the coast. Maybe with kids." He grins. "A baby on the way gives a man a whole new sense of purpose."

I incline my head. They leaked the news at the wedding that Ariana's pregnant. They both wanted to get started on a family right away. Dylan, as the oldest, always had that family-man thing going on. I mean, he might look badass riding around on his Harley with his tribal tattoo designed specifically to showcase his bulging bicep, but he always looked out for us younger brothers. Definitely father material. I stare at him, a strange ache in my chest. It's not that I envy him. I guess I just thought I'd be moving into that part of my life by now too. I'm thirty-one, and I come from a large loving family. I really thought when I committed to Winnie, that was going to be it. Married, house, maybe a dog, kids down the line. I've already had my share of tomcatting around. Speaking of…

My brothers arrive in a bunch like they met up on the street and talked for a bit before wandering in—Jack, Connor, Brendan, and Garrett. People in the neighborhood always say you can tell a Rourke son right away since we resemble our dad—most of us six feet or so, same athletic build, thick dark brown hair, sharp cheekbones, and square jaw. We got our mom's blue eyes, except Garrett. He has aquamarine eyes like our dad.

Jack looks bleary like he had a wild weekend. He's on the quiet side, but don't let that fool you, because it's just to cover up his devious planning for his next prank. And he loves a good party. He's the one egging everyone else on to the next level of craziness. Next in line is Connor. My parents always say Connor was such an angel that they had a fifth child, Brendan. He shocked them being such a mischievous little devil. Garrett, the youngest at twenty-three, is overly muscled from his workouts, so we call him Beast.

"Ya hungover?" I ask Jack loudly just to harass him. My brothers and I always give each other shit.

"I wish," he says. "Neighbor upstairs got a yappy dog that won't shut up. Keeping me up at night." He shoves a hand in his rumpled hair. "I'm gonna have to move. Hey, maybe I'll crash at your place. You've got Winnie's house to yourself, right?"

"It's a construction zone."

"I don't care about that. I'll work around it."

I do *not* want Jack there. He'll want Josie. Any man would, and I can't witness them on their way to a hookup, or after, which is all Jack's ever interested in. "I already have a guest, and there's no more space."

"Who?"

"No one you know."

He smirks. "Did you bring a woman into your ex's place? Does Winnie know? Ha! Ultimate fuck you."

"It's not a fuck you. It's her cousin, and Winnie told her to stay there." I immediately realize my mistake in explaining the situation. Jack is sharp.

"So it *is* a woman."

I blow out a breath. "Yeah." I wait for the harassment. My younger brothers have been saying I need to get back on the horse so I'll relax already. I don't need a woman. I need to finish the renovation.

Jack shakes his head. "You let *her* stay with you, but not your own brother? For shame, bro."

I know he's busting my balls, but I can't help a twinge of guilt. We were raised to have each other's backs. "It's a special situation. She needed to feel safe. You're fine. Besides, she's probably moving out in a week or two."

"Then can I move in?"

"No. I've got inspections and then it goes on the market."

Jack won't shut up about it. "How about me and Winnie's cousin trade? She can stay at my place. It's safe, and she probably won't even hear the dog upstairs. It's mostly a problem because I'm a light sleeper."

"No, she needs to stay put. No trades."

He glances around to our brothers, who I just now realize are listening in. "What's so special about her?" he drawls. "No trades. She *has* to stay put." He smirks.

Deny, deny, deny. "Nothing."

"Have you met her?" Jack asks Connor.

"First time I'm hearing about her," Connor says with a grin.

Jack turns to Brendan and Beast. They shrug.

He turns back to me, a wicked gleam in his eye. "So, Seanie-boy, what's your new female roommate like?"

I lift one shoulder. "I dunno."

Jack smiles widely, which is never good. "Surely, you noticed *something* about this woman who *has* to stay with you."

I play it cool, giving only obvious traits anyone would notice. "She's an actress, red hair, helpful."

Jack pounces. "How is she helpful?" He exchanges an amused look with my brothers.

Heat creeps up my neck. Why did I say that? It sounds like sex stuff. "Not like that. She helps with the renovation."

He cocks his head. "So Winnie's cousin knows construction?"

"No, she's just trying. Really hard. I don't know why." I help myself to coffee, giving them my back and hoping they'll drop it. I take a sip of coffee, ignoring the fact that the room is silent, and I can feel my brothers' curious stares.

"Are ya paying her to help?"

I turn to Brendan. "No."

He lifts a palm. "Duh. She's trying really hard to be helpful because she's into you."

It doesn't matter if she wants me, or if I want her. What matters is that I don't get burned.

"Whatever," I mumble, heat creeping into my cheeks. Hopefully my thick stubble hides the telltale sign of embarrassment. "I took off today to work on the reno, but just wanted to check in. What's the latest?" I turn to Dylan, eager to change the subject.

"Okay," Dylan says. "Now that—"

Jack's voice cuts in. "Men, we've got a situation."

My brothers all talk at once. "We gotta get to Sean's place tonight."

"Yeah."

"Gotta meet her."

"He's blushing, for fuck's sake!"

I hold up a palm. "Nobody's going to my place! I need to work, and she's probably going out." I'm grasping at straws.

"Tomorrow night, then," Jack says.

I set my jaw. "She goes out every night."

Jack's brows draw down. "Where does she go?"

I take in my brothers, who seem way too interested in the corner I've painted myself into. "Different places. Why does it matter?"

Jack smirks, addressing my brothers. "Someone is extremely touchy about this helpful red-haired actress roommate." They snicker. He turns back to me. "Is she like Winnie?"

"Not at all, thankfully," I say way too enthusiastically and quickly backpedal. "Not that I compare them. Can we please talk about something else?"

Dylan pipes up. "I'm thinking of trading in my Harley for a car."

"No-o-o!" Jack protests.

"Blasphemy!" I say. He's been riding Harleys since he was seventeen. This is his second one, and he keeps them in pristine condition. Dylan is synonymous with Harley-riding badass.

Dylan smiles, his blue eyes sparkling with good humor. "Guys, I can't put a baby on the back of my bike."

"Get a sidecar for the bike," Brendan says.

"For a baby?" Dylan asks incredulously. "Have ya heard of car seats?"

"Why don't ya keep the bike *and* get a car?" I ask. It's the end of an era if Dylan becomes one of those station-wagon guys, and I think we all take that a little personally. We always looked to his example as a cool laid-back guy.

"No point," Dylan says. "I'm probably gonna need two cars so Ariana and I can both have a safe ride for the baby whenever we need it. Guys, it's time."

I bow my head. "Moment of silence for the end of an era."

Dylan barks out a laugh. So much for the solemn occasion.

"Can I have your bike?" Beast asks.

Dylan jerks his chin at him. "Make me an offer."

They work it out in a few minutes. Garrett gets the Harley in exchange for his sporty black Mazda outfitted with a wicked stereo system. Not a bad trade. And at least we don't have to witness Dylan driving a station wagon. Next thing you know, he'll have a dad bod, droopy dad jeans, and be telling corny jokes.

Dylan brings us the welcome news that the permits cleared, so we can break ground on developing the former elementary school property into commercial office space. It's our first big development project under Rourke Management. My brothers and I are co-owners of Byrne Construction, the original company, as well as the new development branch. That makes us all invested in its success. The cool thing about our new project is we're also going to put in new playground equipment that's wheelchair-accessible (and still fun for kids not in wheelchairs) and landscape the rest of the lot as a park. It's all part of our development initiative to build parks and playgrounds into it. We want to give back and be part of building neighborhoods. I've been wanting to get into real estate development for a long time, and I'm psyched about our new venture.

The rest of the crew arrives, and I linger at Dylan's signal to wait while he reviews the task list for the day. He wraps up, and everyone heads out to the trucks to drive over to the site. The two of us stay put.

Once we're alone, he says, "When the baby comes, I'm gonna be taking some time off. You're my second-in-command when I'm out. That good by you?"

"Yeah, of course." Dylan and I are tight, only two years apart, and we shared a room growing up. He always leans on me.

He clasps my shoulder. "Thanks. I really appreciate it. You're my go-to guy. I'll breathe easier with you at the reins. And I'll make sure you can legally sign off on financial stuff."

"I got your back. Don't give it a second thought."

Pride has me standing taller as I walk out. I'm committed to my family business, and it means a lot that my older brother knows he can count on me.

By the afternoon, I'm feeling optimistic about the renovation. The counter guys showed up on time, and now the fourth-floor bathroom is finished. Just have to let the glue dry for twenty-four hours. I'm making great progress on the third-floor bathroom too. If I work late tonight, I think I can get to the kitchen demo first thing tomorrow morning.

I'm glad to be busy. It's easier to ignore the draw of Josie, who's still shadowing me. Who am I kidding? She's impossible to ignore, especially when she keeps complimenting me on my neck, shoulders, and back. "Powerful lines of muscular perfection" is probably my favorite. I suppose it's her way of flirting, or maybe she just wants a reaction. Either way, I'm not rising to the bait. I've got work to do and no time for a woman, even if she's sexy and constantly in reach.

Finish the job and move on.

Hell, I never should've kissed her back. It was a mistake, and clearly it encouraged her to want more from me. I'm not going there. Don't have time for complicated relationships.

I pick up a box that was just delivered and take it up to the fourth floor. It's a replacement sconce I've been waiting for to switch out the cracked one in the fourth-floor bathroom. The door to the nearby bedroom is open, and I spot Josie setting her pillow and blanket on the floor as she talks on the phone in a cheerful tone. I told her to move up here before the kitchen demo.

"Everything's good," she says. "No worries." And then she says something that stops me in my tracks. "He finished the top-floor bathroom. Third-floor bathroom is looking great, walls painted, toilet and vanities in."

I step closer, careful to stay out of sight.

"Mmm-hmm. He just needs to add lighting fixtures and towel bars. Then he'll call for the counters to be installed. He starts on the kitchen tomorrow morning." She pauses, listening. "I'm not sure. I'll find out. I think he goes back to his day job on Monday." Pause. "Of course I'll keep you posted!" She goes on with an update on her lack of auditions and how hard it is to wait to hear about the pilot.

I go cold. Now I know the real reason Josie is here—spying for Winnie. And to think I was starting to think Josie was good company. No wonder she shadowed me all week. She went behind my back, just like Winnie. What is it with this family? Slippery as eels.

She says goodbye and steps out of the room.

"Who was that?" Though I'm sure I know. I want her to admit it.

She jumps and puts a hand to her heart. "Skulk much?"

"Spy much?"

Her cheeks flush pink. "Winnie just wanted an update."

"She asked you to spy on me. That's the real reason you're here, isn't it?"

She grimaces, looking guilty as hell. "It was both. I needed a place to crash, and she wanted me to report back on your progress."

"Why didn't she just ask me herself?"

"I told you she was tired of your grumpiness." At my scowl, she adds, "I only said good things about you!"

I speak through my teeth. "That's because there *are* only good things. I thought she trusted me to get the work done right."

"She does! She totally does! It's just her fiancé is pressuring her to sell, so she was considering hiring another contractor if it was too much for you. She knows you have a second job."

I'm so furious I can barely speak. I'm *killing* myself to get this job done. "Don't try to make it sound like this was to make things easier on me. She wants me out, and she doesn't want to feel guilty for firing me." Especially after the way she left me, I add silently. It was an abrupt horrible surprise. Winnie knows she's in the wrong where I'm concerned. The least she could do is let me finish what I started.

She steps closer. "I'm sorry. I didn't think it was a big deal since I was only planning to say good stuff about you. I'd never jeopardize someone's job unless they were a criminal or something."

"Wow, thanks so much. That makes it all better."

"I don't want you to leave anytime soon. I haven't slept so well in a year."

My lip curls. "Well, as long as you can sleep at night." I narrow my eyes as it occurs to me what else she's been up to. "You purposely slowed me down with your constant…friendliness." I refuse to admit it's her sexiness that's a distraction. I'm too pissed at her. She betrayed me just like her cousin. I should've known they'd be working together behind my back. I can't even kick her out since she has more right to be here than I do. It's her grandmother's house. But I want to so badly.

"Sean—"

I hold up a palm. "I'm finishing this job, and then I hope to never see either one of you again."

"Wait. Come on."

I ignore her and head to the bathroom. *Finish the job. Get out.* I open the box and carefully slide out the new frosted glass sconce.

"Sean, I swear I wasn't trying to ruin your job."

Of course she followed me in here. She still needs to report back on every damn thing I do.

"Go away," I snap.

"I'll help you make the work go faster. You want me to

empty out the kitchen cabinets? Clear the space for the demo? Anything you need."

I turn to her, keeping my voice low and controlled. "What I need is for you to go away."

She worries her lower lip, and I focus on installing the sconce. I can feel her watching me, like usual, except this time it's not flattering. If I ignore her long enough, she'll get bored and go away. Though, so far, nothing has put her off hanging with me.

I have plenty of good reasons to keep my distance—she spied on me, she's leaving soon, and I don't need to get burned again. I'm done with her.

"I still think you're an uber-skilled construction worker," she finally says.

I keep my focus on my work, clamping my mouth shut against the harsh thing I want to say. I'm so pissed I can't even look at her right now.

"I'll empty out the kitchen, okay? I can't mess that up. I'll just put stuff in boxes. Do you have any boxes?"

I turn a murderous glare on her. *Sure, I'll drop everything to find you some boxes. Then you can report back to Winnie how slow my progress is.*

She swallows visibly. "I'll come up with something."

I finish up and notice it's quiet downstairs. I'm sure she's going to try to make herself useful, because that's what she does, whether I want her to or not. I'm not going to check on her, even though her history in the kitchen is disastrous. The whole thing will be demolished tomorrow, so how much worse could she make it?

By the time I finish in the third-floor bathroom, I have a plan to get rid of Josie. She likes to think of me as her guard, but I don't want to be her muscle anymore. Not that I ever did anything but exist in her space. I pull my phone out and call my cousin Silvia. She's from the royal side of the family, a princess, who lives in the city with her husband, and guess what? She has a guard. Palace rules. He lives in a nearby apartment and shadows her whenever she goes out. If I can get Silvia to let Josie crash on her couch, she'll feel safe with an actual guard nearby. Some part of me can't leave Josie unprotected, even if I do want to pawn her off on someone else.

"Hello," she answers warmly. Silvia is the nicest person I've ever met. I credit her as the main reason the two sides of our family reconciled. She connected with my family here when she was a student at Yale and worked her magic to get us all invited back to Villroy for her twin, Adrian's wedding.

"Hey, Sil. How're ya?"

"I'm doing well, thank you. I just got back in town yesterday. It was a lovely wedding, wasn't it?"

"It was great. I, uh, was wondering if you could do me a favor."

"Absolutely."

"Don't ya wanna know what it is?"

"I'll do anything in my power to help out family."

So damn nice. "I really appreciate that. I told ya how I'm renovating Winnie's place in my spare time, and now I've got a tight deadline. So, Winnie's cousin showed up here 'bout a week ago to crash on my couch. She needs to feel safe with a guard. Do ya think she could crash with you since you have a guard? She's slowing me down here, and I need to focus."

"I don't understand. If she needs a guard, what's she doing there?"

Spying on me, distracting me, tempting me. I can't say any of that without making her sound like a person you don't want on your couch. I need to sell her good points. "I guess Winnie thought I fit the bill as guard since I'm big and protective. Josie just needs to feel safe, but I don't think I'm the guy for that. I'm not exactly trained as a guard, and I'm busy."

"Is someone stalking her?"

"No. She just had a bad experience with an aggressive guy."

"Is he still a danger to her?"

I rub the back of my neck. "No. He's in LA. But she's vulnerable. She'd do much better at your place with your guard."

"Hmm…"

"Sil, she can't stay here. She's a distraction."

"So first she's vulnerable and now she's a distraction. What's the real problem?"

I hesitate, not wanting to admit the truth.

"Sean, I can't help you if I don't know the whole story. Is it because she's Winnie's cousin?" Her voice takes on a sympathetic tone. "Does she remind you of Winnie and it brings back bad memories? I know sometimes it can be hard to get over an ex, especially one that betrayed—"

I can't take the sympathy. "She's spying on me! My ex planted her here to report on my progress. She admitted it!"

"Wow, she's really got you riled up. I don't think I've ever heard you so out of sorts, even when Winnie walked out on you and, if ever there was a time to be riled, it was then."

My lips press in a flat line. So much for nice Silvia making my life easier. "Look, I can't kick her out. It's not my house. Can ya help me out?"

"Bring her for Sunday dinner at my place. We'll chat, and I'll introduce her to Leon to see if a guard is really what she wants."

"Thank you." *Finally* she's helping me. I'm sure Leon will look appropriately menacing with his earpiece, stone-faced expression, and concealed weapon. Now that's real protection. And I won't have to be tempted by an untrustworthy woman. I've already been burnt by her cousin.

"No problem," Silvia says cheerily. "See you both soon!"

I thank her again and hang up, a weight lifted from my shoulders. Now I'll just grab a bite to eat and take the night off before the hard work of demo tomorrow. By the end of the weekend, my problem will be solved. I head downstairs to the kitchen, expecting a disaster area, but it's neat. Boxes are lined up by the couch across the room and neatly labeled in black marker. She emptied the kitchen cabinets for me.

She's not here. My shoulders droop. Do I actually miss her?

I shake it off and go to the refrigerator in case there's still leftovers. We split a noodle dish last night. No noodles, but there's a new dinner waiting for me—a large wrapped chicken parmigiana sub with a masking tape label that reads "your dinner." Something in the vicinity of my heart swells. That was really thoughtful of her.

I take out my dinner, settle at the island, and eat. It's too quiet. I got used to eating dinner with her cheery conversation. Guilt seeps in. It's not Josie's fault that Winnie put her in such a difficult position, asking her to spy. I was too hard on Josie, taking out my anger with Winnie on her. And now Josie went out, and I don't know where. I don't know what time she'll be back, or if she's safe. Hell, she got to me. I did everything in my power to hold her at a distance, but she wormed her way in. I don't want to care if she's okay. I don't want to care about any woman. I just want to keep my head down, do my work, make a success of myself, and then I'll think about dating again. This'll all be so much better once Josie is safely living with Silvia and her guard. It's only for a couple more weeks, anyway, until Josie flies off for her next job.

I finish my dinner, which doesn't taste as good as it normally would because I can't help but think I drove Josie away. Now all I want is for her to come back so I can stop wondering if she's okay. I snag my laptop from upstairs and return to the couch, shoving a box out of the way with my foot. There's only four boxes from the kitchen since it was just my stuff. I browse for a movie on the laptop, but nothing appeals. It's Friday night. I should go out. I deserve a night out after all my hard work.

The door opens, and Josie steps inside, carrying a brown bag. "I got some beer, roomie."

I smile, relief flooding me. She's okay, and she brought a peace offering. "Thanks, and thanks for packing up the kitchen and for dinner too. That was a real help."

"You're welcome. I ate the noodles, but I thought you'd need protein to keep up those muscles."

My chest puffs out over the compliment. I guess I kinda got used to her compliments.

She heads for the kitchen, setting the bag on the island. I join her, watching as she pulls two beers out and puts the rest in the refrigerator.

She turns to me. "I think I packed the bottle opener."

"I got it." I lever the bottle open using the edge of the island counter and hand her the first beer before doing the same for my own.

"So we're cool?" she asks.

"Yeah. I was hard on you earlier, more mad at Winnie than you."

She waves that away. "No, it's fine. I should've been up front and told you Winnie asked me to report on your progress."

"She put you in a bad position. Just don't do it again, okay? I'll give her progress updates."

"I wasn't going to. I felt bad about it, even though I was saying good things."

"I'm over it. You wanna watch a movie?"

"Sure!"

After a short debate on the merits of old black-and-white romantic comedies (her favorite) and superhero movies (mine), we agree on a thriller. Before I hit play, I tell her, "My cousin Silvia invited me to dinner on Sunday night. She said you're welcome to join us."

Her eyes widen. "You mean Princess Silvia?"

I settle back on the couch next to her. "Yeah. You'll like her. She's really nice."

"Wow. Dinner with a princess. I'd love to. Did you tell her about me?"

"Yeah. I mentioned I had a guest."

"It was nice of her to invite me."

I ignore the stab of guilt over the real reason for the dinner, pawning her off on another guard. "Yeah, well, that's Silvia."

I put the movie on and set the laptop on top of some boxes so we can both see it. I shouldn't feel guilty. I'm only sending Josie away for her own good. I won't snap at her if she's not here, and I'm sure she'll feel a lot safer with an armed guard trained to fend off an attacker instead of just me. I'm not trained beyond holding my own with my brothers and the occasional playground bully. Josie needs to feel safe, and that's exactly what she'll be with Silvia.

She smiles at me, and my chest warms. "I'm glad we're back on the right footing."

"Yeah, sure," I mutter and take a long swallow of beer.

Then I focus on the movie. Not her sweet fruity floral scent, not her contented sigh, and definitely not her pink lips wrapped around that bottle. I'm stronger than that.

6

<hr>

I'm still a little hazy on why Princess Silvia would include me in a family dinner, but I've concluded it must be Sean's version of a peace offering. He wants to introduce me to someone interesting and also spend time with me outside our construction-zone home. I'd go so far as to say Sean and I are friends now. After the movie on Friday night, we talked about all of the plot holes in it, and we laughed a lot. He was actually fun with a great sense of humor. Last night he was working on the kitchen, but he did invite me to join him for a quick dinner at a pizzeria down the block. The relaxed version of Sean is irresistible.

I can admit it. I want more of that, more of him. We had one really nice kiss, and tonight feels like a fresh start with him inviting me to dinner with his family. I can't help but think it's a little bit like a date and maybe something could happen between us. I know it's weird with him being Winnie's ex, but she gave up any rights to him when she cheated on him. An affair of the heart is just as bad as a hookup. She let herself have feelings for Colin before she ended it with Sean. That's wrong.

I pull a tissue from my purse, blot my red lipstick, and add a second layer. I'm wearing a cute black polka-dot minidress with tiny pearl buttons lined up the front of it. And I've got my red purse that perfectly matches my slip-on red suede heels. I like to use red pops of color to go with my dyed red hair. I toss my lipstick in my purse. Okay, I'm ready for dinner out with my roomie. And potentially more.

I zip my purse closed and stand there for a moment as it occurs to me I'm leaving soon. I could hear as early as this Friday about the pilot. That's not fair to Sean to start something. I get the feeling he's at a point in his life where he's looking for something a little more serious. It makes sense. He had that recently with Winnie, and he's a grounded responsible guy in his thirties. I dig that. Most guys I meet are immature. It's not like Sean would ever move to LA to be with me, where I'll most likely end up. He's rooted in Brooklyn with his family-owned construction and real estate development business. Not exactly the kind of job that travels. And I know from personal experience, long distance is hard. I tried it with my college boyfriend, and things fell apart within two weeks. Probably didn't help that he hooked up with his costar in a play in London right away. For guys, it's out of sight, out of mind.

Okay, so friends. No problem.

I head downstairs to find Sean waiting for me on the parlor floor, where he sleeps, and catch his look of open admiration before his expression turns carefully neutral. My heart thumps harder, my breath quickening. He's unaware I'm a student of human emotion—all part of my acting toolbox. He's dressed nicely in a light blue button-down dress shirt with tan trousers and brown leather shoes. Clean-shaven, too, for the first time ever. He has sharp cheekbones and a square jaw. A classically handsome face. His thick dark brown hair is still a little damp from the shower. He must've showered outside because I was hogging the upstairs shower.

I'm drawn to him, like always, and walk right into his personal space. I feel comfortable enough to do that when he's not scowling at me, and I want to be closer to him. All the reasons to keep my distance fade in my mind.

"You look nice," I tell him.

He clears his throat and shoves his hands in his pockets. "Thanks. You too."

"Is the car here?" His cousin arranged for her driver to pick us up. Must be nice to be royalty. Too bad Sean didn't get any of those perks, being part of the exiled family.

"Yeah, it's out front. Ready?"

"Sure."

He gestures for me to go ahead of him. I head downstairs and carefully tread across the drop cloths he put down on this floor. The kitchen is gone except for the refrigerator, which he left plugged in against the far wall until the new one gets here. He holds my elbow, surprising me, as he guides me out the door. Up until now, he never purposely touched me. Except for that one kiss I sort of coaxed him into. Warmth spreads from my elbow straight up my arm.

A black Mercedes with tinted windows waits on the street. The driver gets out, wearing a white dress shirt and black trousers, and greets us warmly, holding the back door open for us.

I slip inside first, and Sean joins me. After the car pulls away from the curb, I lean close and whisper, "Do you travel like this a lot?"

He answers in a low voice, "Never. Silvia surprised me offering her driver. Maybe it's because I'm bringing a guest."

"A female guest." I nudge him with my elbow. "She probably thinks I'm your girlfriend."

"No. I didn't tell her that."

"She assumed it since I live with you."

"Trust me, she doesn't think that. I told her you were Winnie's cousin temporarily crashing on the couch."

I lean my head back on the seat, hiding my disappointment. Clearly he's not as into me as I'm into him. "Well, whatever reason she had, it sure beats the subway."

"Yeah," he mutters, looking out the window.

"Everything okay?"

"Yup," he says tightly.

I suppress a sigh. I've spent a lot of time with Sean over the past week, and I can tell he's got something on his mind.

He's got two modes—intense focused work mode and relaxed nonwork mode. I only glimpsed nonwork mode briefly. This tight work deadline must be a real strain on him.

"You're making great progress on the renovation," I say.

"Yeah, but I have to go back to my day job tomorrow, so that's gonna slow me down."

"I can do stuff for you while you're gone. Prep something, maybe?"

"No!"

"Geez, you don't have to shout at me. I can be helpful."

He lifts a palm. "You are at certain things. Please don't touch anything when I'm not home."

"Okay, okay."

"Any news on the pilot yet?"

"No, I won't hear until the end of this week at the earliest. I have an audition for a car insurance commercial tomorrow though. Fingers crossed."

"That's something."

"Yeah, it's not like my dream job, obviously, but it can be a good payday for a day's work, plus I get paid a residual every time it airs, and that keeps money in the bank while I pursue better jobs. I've been living off my perfume commercial for the past four months. It was a national spot that aired a lot this past Christmas. I can probably stretch that money out for a year if I'm frugal."

"I don't think I saw it."

"You probably tuned it out. It's not like you knew who I was at the time. It was a fun shoot at a mini-golf course. Later, they digitally edited the perfume bottle to be the ball. I got a hole in one, of course, with the magic of editing. I had one line, 'Ready to play?' said in a sexy playful voice." I try it out on him. "Ready to play?"

He stares at me and licks his lips. "I, uh, can see why ya booked it."

"Thanks!" *Me thinks he likes the sexy.*

"It must be tough not knowing when your next paycheck is coming."

"Yeah, I traded security for my dream. But I always think positive that my big break is just around the corner."

He looks thoughtful. "I guess that's what ya hafta tell yourself. At what point do ya say, enough, I'm getting a regular job?"

"Never."

"It could happen. The bank account gets low. Ya get tired of crashing on people's couches."

"I'm young! I'm not worried about it. I'll get there."

"Okay." He sounds unconvinced.

"I do get parts, you know. I have a BFA in drama, and I've been in a ton of theater."

"Paying theater?"

I bristle. "Watch my reel if you want to see me in action. You'll see I know what I'm doing."

"It's not that I doubt ya. I just think it's a really tough way to earn a living."

"Well, someone has to. The entertainment industry exists for a reason." I pull out my phone and text him the link to my website. "Check it out later."

He does right away, which I hadn't expected.

"I said later," I tell him. "Not in front of me."

He presses pause on it. "Why? You perform for an audience. What's the difference?"

"The difference is I can't usually watch myself at the same time as someone else watches me. I don't want to know if you don't like it."

"I'll put on my poker face." He presses play again, and I can tell right away he's confused by something. He doesn't know how well I can read him.

"What?"

He shifts, giving me his back.

I can hear it playing, and I so wish I hadn't been so defensive I had to prove myself. Why do I care what he thinks? It's only a three-minute reel, but it's the longest three minutes of my life.

He turns back to me. "You're good."

I let out a breath. "Thank you. And you're good at your job too."

"I know."

"Just say thank you!" I say on a laugh.

He smiles the best kind of smile that reaches his blue eyes, his handsome face lighting up. "Thanks, Josie."

By the time we arrive at Silvia's place, I'm in a great mood. Sean and I seem to have gelled. He filled me in on his family, the scandalous break in it, and the close-knit family he has in Brooklyn. The way he describes his brothers' antics growing up and their camaraderie now on the job, all working together in the family business, I'm actually a little jealous. I'm close with my parents, but I never got that big-family experience or the fun sibling experience. He's really grounded by family with deep roots here. I'm not sure I'll ever have roots. I have to go wherever the job is.

Silvia answers the door with a serious-looking man standing behind her entirely in black. "Hello! Welcome!" She's young, probably close to my age, with a very girl-next-door vibe. Her dark brown hair falls in a soft wave just past her shoulders, bare minimum of makeup, her hazel eyes warm as they take us both in. She's wearing a cute black and white striped dress with tan gladiator sandals. I was worried she'd be a little aloof, being a royal, but she seems like someone I'd hang with anytime.

"Thank you," I say. "It's so great to meet you."

"Hey, Sil," Sean says. "Thanks for having us over."

She steps back so we can come in and goes up on tiptoe to kiss Sean's cheek. "So nice to have you both!" she exclaims, thrusting her hand out to me. "I'm Silvia."

I shake her hand. "I'm Josie."

She beams. "Usually I go out to Brooklyn, but Sean wanted to see me all by himself without all his gruff and growly brothers."

I grin. "You mean they're grumpier than he is?"

"I wouldn't say grumpy. More like deep growly voices. All bark, don't worry." She gestures to the man standing just past her shoulder in a black blazer, black T-shirt, and black trousers. "This is my guard, Leon."

"Hi, nice to meet you," I say.

Sean nods at him.

Leon inclines his head slightly. No smile. Brr...is it chilly in here?

"You're in luck," Silvia says. "My husband, Cade, is making his famous ultimate lasagna. Well, famous in our house." She gestures for us to follow her to the kitchen, where a man with longish dirty blond hair, a full beard, and a ready smile is slicing tomatoes for a salad. "Cade, this is Josie. And you know my cousin."

Cade wipes his hand on his apron and shakes my hand before turning to Sean. "Good to see you again, Sean. What's it been, a week?"

"Yeah." Sean turns to me. "He was at my brother's wedding in Villroy."

"Big family turnout," Silvia says, looking pleased. "Can I get you some wine? I have a really nice Italian red."

"Sure," I say. Out of the corner of my eye, I spot Leon the guard hovering in the doorway of the kitchen. Does he think I'm a threat? Stand down! I'm a peace-loving woman.

Cade points at Sean. "I got you, man. Beer's in the fridge."

"Thanks," Sean says, helping himself to a beer.

"Let's go to the living room," Silvia says. "Dinner won't be long."

She leads the way, and Leon trails behind her. The rest of us follow her to a seating area with a brown suede sofa, two turquoise chairs, and a glass coffee table. There's a wall of windows facing Central Park. We're on the top floor, so it's a gorgeous view. Across from the large living room is a dining area with a black wood table and six matching chairs.

She takes a seat on the sofa with Cade, and Leon stands behind her at a slight angle. He's like her shadow. Does he live with them? That must be strange for a married couple. How can you have spontaneous sex with a skulking shadow?

Sean and I take the chairs across from them.

"So, Josie, you're new in town, right?" Silvia asks.

"Kinda. I lived here for college. I alternate New York and LA for auditions."

"She's an actress," Sean says. "Really talented."

I turn to him, smiling. "Thank you."

"Oh, isn't that exciting?" Silvia enthuses. "Would I have seen you in anything?"

"I was in the Blossom perfume commercial this past holiday season. I was playing mini golf, and the perfume was supposed to be the ball."

"I know that one! You were wearing a bright yellow dress. How cute!" She turns to Cade. "You remember that commercial?"

"Vaguely. I probably checked my phone when it came on if it was for perfume. No offense."

"No offense taken," I say.

"Anything else I might've seen you in?" she asks with a smile.

I keep my smile firmly in place. "Not unless you're a middle-school kid watching an educational series about library resources."

"Ha! No."

"She did a pilot," Sean puts in.

I smile at him. "Yes. I'm excited about it. If it gets picked up, I could be in a sitcom for at least a season."

"It films in LA," Sean says. "She could be leaving in a week or two. The earliest she'll hear is the end of this week."

I send him a sideways look. Strange that he's speaking on my behalf when I'm sitting right here.

He pulls out his phone. "Check out her video clip on her website."

I flush. "No need to watch."

"I want to," Silvia says. "Don't be shy. Sean already sang your praises."

Sean makes a face. "I didn't sing her praises. Objectively speaking, she's talented."

"Nothing personal, right?" Silvia says, giving me a wink. "Let me see."

Sean hands over his phone, and I try not to squirm as

Silvia and Cade watch it together. Leon remains standing stoically behind Silvia, staring straight ahead. It's like partying with a statue. So strange. If I ever get famous, I guess I'll need a guard too. I'm going to make mine keep a distance away. Upstairs a level from me, or downstairs. Easy to reach if I scream for help, but not hovering.

Silvia hands back Sean's phone when the video finishes. "Very cool, Josie. I liked the contrast in scenes too, with drama and comedy. Which is your favorite?"

"I like everything. I want to be one of those actors not defined by genre, you know? Like, I could be in an action adventure, a rom-com, or a thriller. Like Claire Jordan."

Silvia tilts her head. "I know her. Well, I don't know her personally, but my US wedding planner also planned Claire Jordan's wedding. Maybe I could touch base with her about connecting you two."

I suck in air. "Omigod. That would be amazing. Claire Jordan is my idol! She's done so many genres, so many fantastic roles, and she has her own production company. Just to meet her and talk to her about her experience would be such an honor."

"Wonderful!" Silvia exclaims. "Give me your number, and I'll be in touch if Claire's available."

I shoot Sean a *can you believe this* look before turning back to her. "I'm sure she's so busy. She just had a new movie come out, and I know she has two kids now, Owen and Harper. Plus she has her production company, Red Jewel Films."

They all stare at me.

I lift one shoulder up and down. "I've done a little research. Every time I find an actress with a career I admire, I try to figure out how she got there. You know, follow her career steps. The personal stuff is just there alongside it." I laugh. "Okay, I'm a total fangirl!"

"I'll text you Josie's contact info," Sean says to Silvia before I can do it on my own. He taps his phone and sends it. He sure is being proactive on my behalf tonight. It feels good to know he wants me to succeed. It means he believes in me.

Silvia sends him a curious look before turning to me and smiling sweetly. "I hope it turns out to be a good connection."

"I so appreciate it," I gush.

She smiles and takes a sip of wine. "So, Josie, how's it going with my cousin for a roommate?"

I beam at Sean. "Great! We know how to work around each other, and I've got no complaints."

Sean tugs at his collar. "It's been an adjustment. I'm used to working solo, but Josie…she's there too."

I stiffen. "I'm there too?"

He grimaces, looking away.

My mood tanks, and I swallow hard. "I thought you said I helped you. And I do make sure you have dinner every night."

He lowers his voice. "I think I can handle takeout on my own. Besides, it's not a good living situation with all the construction debris."

I narrow my eyes. After all I've done for him? "So I'm just an annoyance?"

Cade excuses himself to check on dinner. Silvia watches Sean closely. So do I. Here I was feeling so warmly toward him when he resented my very existence.

"Well?" I prompt. "Just say what you really think of me."

He exhales sharply, throws Silvia a beseeching look, who gestures for him to go on, and turns back to me. "Okay, fine. You're a distraction. I said that from the beginning. I need focus. I wasn't supposed to have a roommate. I only let you stay because Winnie said you needed to feel safe."

"Is Sean your makeshift guard?" Silvia asks me. "He's not carrying a weapon, you know. Unlike Leon."

I glance over at the menacing Leon, who slides his blazer back to reveal a gun. I gulp. "I don't need that much protection."

Sean takes a long pull of his beer, staring straight ahead. Something is off.

Silvia smiles. "That may be true, but if Sean's getting on your nerves, you're welcome to crash here. Leon can look after both of us."

My jaw drops, and I turn to Sean, who pastes on a fake smile. "That's a nice offer," he says.

Did Princess Silvia just invite me to crash with her five minutes after meeting me? And why doesn't Sean look in the least surprised? And then I know—he tried to pawn me off on her! The rat! That's the whole reason I'm here. This is the thanks I get after all I've done to help him! I feed the big jerk, I clean up after his dishes, and…I wiped down an entire bathroom! That was hard work. I handed him tools and fetched lots of tile, running up and down several flights of stairs. Not to mention emptying out the kitchen for him! If that makes me a bother, then he doesn't deserve me.

"I've done a lot for you," I tell Sean in a choked voice. Dammit. My eyes are hot. I turn to Silvia. "Excuse me, where's your bathroom?"

She gives me a sympathetic look and points. "Just down the hall."

I jump up and rush there before Sean can see how upset I am. I don't want to be upset over him. I don't want to care about him at all. I wish I didn't. He grew on me with his gruff competent ways and the occasional glimpse into a man who seemed to run deep. That kiss had me imagining more than was really there.

I give myself a pep talk in the mirror and then do a deep-breathing exercise to reach calm again. I've had plenty of practice in settling myself before auditions. Sure, this is worse because it's personal, but the same principles apply. I. Am. Fine. I *will* be fine.

When I return to the living room, Silvia says, "Sorry, Josie. Leon doesn't feel comfortable extending security to another person. He says we'd need to hire another guard for you."

"That's okay. I don't need a guard."

"You still need to feel safe," Sean says.

"Don't worry about me," I say through my teeth.

"What about staying with my parents?" he asks. "My dad's a big guy, and they've got room."

I use my coolest, most composed voice. "No need. I'll find another place to crash as soon as I can manage it."

"With who?" Sean demands.

"I don't know," I fire back. "Maybe someone from my improv class."

"A guy?"

Why does he care as long as I'm out of his hair?

I shoot Sean a hard look. "We'll talk later."

He grunts. The grouch is back. Who cares? Now I'm grouchy too. I've never felt so unappreciated in my life. And so hurt.

I toss back my wine, draining the glass.

"More wine?" Sophia asks.

"Yes, thank you."

She refills my glass and gives Sean a pointed look. "Maybe you should help Cade get dinner on the table."

Sean flushes guiltily and takes the hint, leaving the room.

The moment he leaves, she leans forward. "He's normally very easygoing with a great wit. He's been under a lot of pressure."

I shake my head. "He's been irritated by my presence right from the beginning. Maybe *one time* he wasn't a complete grump to me. I'm sick of it. I'm done."

She takes a sip of wine and says serenely, "Okay."

"Really. I couldn't be more serious."

"I'm sure."

I bite back a sharp remark. The last thing I want is to fight with Princess Silvia, especially when she agreed to connect me to Claire Jordan. "I heard you're a children's book editor. Is that as fun as it sounds?"

She glances toward the kitchen. "He's a good guy, and he means well. Don't be too hard on him."

I purse my lips. Obviously his cousin is on his side.

7

Sean

Tonight was a disaster. Silvia made dinner go by as smoothly as possible, which was not easy with Josie sending pissy looks at me. Worse, the guilt has been eating me up inside. I think Josie cried in the bathroom. I feel awful about that because Josie doesn't have a mean bone in her body. She's always so open and cheerful. I was only trying to keep some distance for both our sakes.

I can't live with her anymore. I don't know what she expects will happen. There's chemistry. And, okay, fine, I like her. I didn't want to like her, but I do, and she's only going to worm her way in more, and then she's going to leave. And I'm not going anywhere. I can't. My brothers depend on me for our shared business.

We're in the car on our way back home, and Josie hasn't said a word to me since we left Silvia's apartment.

I can't take the silence anymore. "It was only a friendly invitation to use Leon as your guard."

She scowls. "I don't appreciate the way you tried to pawn me off on your cousin. You could've just asked me if I wanted to stay there. Instead, you made this elaborate plan behind my back."

"Silvia had to meet you first, but obviously she liked you enough to invite you to stay with her."

"She took back the invitation two minutes later."

"Because I told her to after I realized you were upset about it."

She looks out the window, silent again.

"Hey, you went behind my back before too. I forgave you."

She turns to me, her eyes narrowing. "I take back every compliment I ever gave you about your neck."

"Fine."

"Your shoulders and back are still a thing of beauty, but that's beside the point. You're my roomie and nothing more."

Some of my guilt eases because she complimented me, which means maybe she's feeling a little better. "That's all I ever was."

"No, you kissed me once."

"You *told* me to."

Her chin juts out. "That was not me. We were doing improv."

No way am I letting her pin that kiss on me. "Call it what ya want, but there was no question you wanted me to kiss you. 'Yes, and kiss me.' Your exact words."

She crosses her arms. "Yes, and never again. I'm designing a new room."

My brows draw together. "What?"

She drops her arms. "Improv. Yes, and…then the other person adds something new."

"Stop with the improv. I don't wanna play games. I just want…" I trail off because I realize what I really want is something that can never work—the two of us, together. "Look, I'll be straightforward with you from here on out, you do the same, and we'll go back to, ya know, friendly roommates."

She stares at me for a long moment, and I hold her stare. I don't know why, but I can't lose this staring contest.

Finally, she says, "Silvia told me you're normally easygoing with a great wit. Boy, was she wrong."

"A great wit? Like I'm funny?"

"Yes. What happened to you?"

"Oh, I don't know, maybe working twenty-four seven with my ex breathing down my neck, and her spying cousin distracting me and slowing me down at every turn has something to do with it."

She jabs a finger at me. "You still haven't forgiven Winnie. That's the real problem here."

The real problem is I *have* forgiven Winnie. I'm over her, but I was burned, and I don't want to get burned again. Josie is leaving for LA soon for her sitcom. There's no question in my mind someone as talented as her will get it. Her personality alone could carry a show. I can avoid entanglement for the next week or two before she heads to LA. I can't say any of that to her because then she'll know I care too much. It'll make it harder to keep my distance.

I go on the defensive. "If I haven't forgiven her, then why would I be fine staying at her place and renovating it?"

She throws her hands up. "I have no idea."

"I'm over her."

"You're not over her."

"This has nothing to do with Winnie. I love the house. I love the neighborhood. I want to see it through."

She waves a hand airily. "That all sounds perfectly reasonable. Unfortunately, I don't believe a word you just said."

My temper flares. "Whatta ya wanna hear? That I thought this was my future, living a different life in Park Slope, and I can't let it go?"

"At least it's honest."

I lean close. "This project means something to me. I've been working on it for more than a year." I pull back. "And, yeah, I want this life, even without her. I'm ambitious. I don't wanna always be just a construction worker. I told ya my family's getting into real estate development. Rourke Management, that's us. Winnie's place will look great in our portfolio. Did you know your grandmother paid five thousand dollars for it in nineteen fifty-three? When I finish this renovation to my standards, it'll go for three million at least."

Her eyes widen. "Whoa. I had no idea."

"Yeah. I'm gonna be a developer. Maybe I'll get into the financial side of it too. Less sweat, more brain power."

She looks at me curiously. "You know finances?"

"I can learn."

"I'm ambitious too. I want to be just like Claire Jordan."

"You shouldn't try to be just like someone else. Just be yourself."

She scoffs. "You say that like I'm actually an okay person, and I know you see me as nothing but a giant inconvenience."

"I'm just sayin', don't be a wannabe Claire Jordan."

She sighs. "Look, I know Winnie really screwed you up, and I'm sorry about that, but please keep me out of the blast zone. I've done nothing but help you since the day we met."

"You set off the smoke detector, made a mess of the kitchen, made me worry about you, and generally made yourself a nuisance."

She sucks in air, blinking rapidly.

I grimace, fearing she's about to cry again on my account. "Not really a nuisance. I take that back."

She meets my gaze directly, her eyes shiny with unshed tears. My gut twists. "No, don't take it back. It's obviously how you really feel about me."

"No, it's not. I shouldn't have said that."

She turns away. I hear a sniffle.

"I like you," I admit. "Even though I don't want to."

She turns to me, blinking back tears. "Why don't you want to like me? Because of Winnie?"

"You're leaving anyway. What does it matter?"

"So if I didn't leave, you'd like me more?"

I face forward, muttering, "You're twisting my words around."

She's quiet for a moment before saying, "I was right about you."

I turn to her. "Right about what?"

"You're a committing kind of man, not a fling kind. I find that refreshing."

"I'm whatever I feel like. I don't have time for the complication of a woman. That's the real reason I want to live alone, but you're always right there."

"Fine, I get it. You don't have to be so harsh. You won't see me. And you can forget me serving you dinner every night."

I shake my head. So weird how she thinks that's such a big help. It's not like she's cooking. "I can manage to eat takeout on my own."

"Good because you're officially on your own from now on."

"Whatta ya mean?"

"I'll go out as much as possible so you won't even know I'm around."

"Great." Only it doesn't feel great. My chest aches. I might've just pushed her so far away she'll never return.

"Besides, I'm probably going to hear back about my pilot soon."

"Hope ya get it."

Her brows lift. "Because I'll leave, or because you wish me well?"

"I don't know how to answer that."

"Would it kill you to be nice to me?"

I exhale sharply. "I don't know where you got the idea that I was nice."

She stares straight ahead, her lips in a flat line.

It occurs to me she'll be going out every *night* since that's the only time I'll be home once I start working at my day job tomorrow. But will I be able to focus if she's out there in the city by herself at night? She doesn't have a tough New Yorker attitude. More like, *hey, let's hang out!*

Before I can help myself, the words are out of my mouth. "Let me know your schedule and text me if you'll be late. I don't wanna waste my time checking if ya got home okay."

Her lips curve up a little before she presses them in a flat line. She doesn't mind when I'm protective. She likes it. "Consider it done. You won't have to waste a second of your time on me."

"Good."

"Do you mind if I have a guest upstairs?"

My jaw clenches. Does she mean a guy or a girl? I can't ask or she'll think I'm jealous, which I am, even though I have no right to be. "No guests. The place is still a construction zone."

"The fourth floor is fine. There's this guy in my improv class who wants to practice more with me."

I study her. Is she yanking my chain? Hard to tell. Her face is the picture of innocence.

"Practice what?" I ask.

"Improv."

"Kissing improv?" That's what she did with me.

She shrugs.

"I think it's a terrible idea, especially when you're leaving so soon."

"Okay." She sounds pleased.

"What's that supposed to mean? Okay?"

She gives me a secret smile. "It means okay."

"You sound like you're implying something more."

"You're hoping I'm implying more, aren't you?"

I clamp my mouth shut before I blurt out the truth—the only reason I want her gone is to eliminate temptation. I have the uneasy feeling she already suspects the truth.

She sighs and leans her head against my shoulder.

I don't push her away.

When I get home after work Monday night, I hear a noise upstairs and find myself hoping it's her, even though she said she plans to go out every night.

"Josie?" I call.

Silence.

I head upstairs, but she's not here. It was just the old house settling. I need to get used to a life without Josie. I'm the one who pushed her away, with good reason, so I just have to deal with the temporary discomfort of not knowing where she is, whom she's with, or when she'll be back. Fuck my life.

I go down to the kitchen, microwave one of the frozen dinners I brought home, which look nothing like the picture on the box, and wolf it down on the back deck. Then I get to work on the kitchen, feeling unsatisfied and unusually cranky.

An hour later, I need to know what's up with her. I pull out my phone and text her, brief and to the point: *Estimated time of arrival?*

No response. What's she doing? Is she with that guy from improv?

I shove my phone in my back jeans pocket and get to work. It vibrates when I'm in the middle of installing a new upper cabinet. I hold the cabinet in place with one hand, set down the drill, and reach for my phone.

Josie: *Be back 9ish. I'm visiting a friend from college. Maybe 10ish. She wants to take me to meet some of her friends in Harlem. We might have a jam session.*

I shove the phone back in my pocket and finish installing the cabinet. Then I pull my phone out again and send her a quick text. *You play an instrument?*

Josie: *I'm passable on the piano.*

Me: *Multitalented. Cool.*

She sends a kiss emoji. Okay, don't get excited. Emojis are casual things. Still, the blood thrums through my veins, suddenly alert.

Josie: *My mother's an opera singer. I grew up with music in my life. Did I ever tell you that?*

Me: *Yeah. I heard you sing once. You were really good.*

Josie: *Wow. So many compliments tonight. I can tap dance too.*

I find myself smiling. Somehow it's easier to say stuff through text.

Me: *That I'd like to see.*

Josie: *Maybe. If you ask really nicely. What's your talent? Besides being an uber-talented construction guy.*

I text back on impulse. *I'm good in bed.*

I grimace. What am I doing?

Shit. She stopped responding. I wish I could take back a text. I look around at the half-finished space as if someone here could help me out. How do I fix this? I'm about to text, *Sorry. Sent that to the wrong person*, when she texts again.

Josie: *Hey, had to respond to my friend. Back to you. Does that count as a talent? Also, inappropriate.*

Me: *It's more a gift than a talent. And that was inappropriate.*

Josie: *Are we sexting?*

I laugh out loud and text back: *Do you want to be sexting?*

Josie: *Maybe. It is super boring on the subway.*

Me: *You don't need to stay away every night. I didn't mean to scare you off.*

Josie: *Why did you?*

I can't tell her the truth and still keep my distance.

Me: *I don't know.*

Josie: *I expect to see good progress in the kitchen when I get back. Let's get this job finished and Winnie out of your hair for good.*

Me: *I hear that. Alright, back to work.*

Josie: *You got this, stud. (Construction humor) :p*

I'm smiling as I text a quick bye. I need to stop snarling at her. I can be civil, friendly even, without getting too close.

I go back to work, a new burst of energy coursing through me. I can't wait to show her how much I've accomplished tonight.

~

Josie

I've been on edge all week, anxious to find out about the pilot. My agent says she's pretty sure we're going to hear something by Friday, which is today. I tell myself if it doesn't work out, then it just wasn't the right project. There's lots of stories about actors who lost one show only to land an even better one that became a smash hit. What's meant to be will be. I kept myself busy this week with auditions (had several for commercials and for a show on a new streaming service), improv class, the gym, and visits to everyone I could think of in the city, including dropping in at NYU to say hey to my fave teachers. I even went to an open-mike night at an alternative comedy club. I did a bit as an overenthusiastic triangle player, who dreams of joining a rock band, because why not? The audience at these shows is looking for something different. I visited Winnie one night too, who seemed unusually tense, though she said it was just wedding-planning stress.

Now it's Friday night, still early enough to hear news from LA, and I'm holed up in my fourth-floor room, trying to tune out Sean with his noisy power tools in the kitchen. He's installing a new island. He texted me every night this week, checking on what time I'd be home. It's clear he cares about me, but what does it matter when he keeps his distance? I sigh. I hate to admit it, but he's probably right to keep his distance, with him being deeply rooted here and me about to fly off at a moment's notice. We only saw each other for a quick hello when I got in every night. He wasn't waiting up for me, he was working in the kitchen. Maybe it's his way of trying to be friendly after he felt bad for acting like I was such an irritating thorn in his side.

One good thing happened this week. I heard back from Claire Jordan, and she invited me to meet at a restaurant in the city next weekend to chat. It gives me hope. If one good thing happened, then don't good things happen in threes? I'm due for two more. I'm throwing all my positive energy out into the world.

My phone rings, and I check the screen, my heart racing. It's my agent. This is it. The big moment. I'll be telling interviewers about the moment I got this show and how exhilarating it was. I jump up and down a few times to expel my nervous energy.

"Hi, Jade!" I answer cheerfully. "Do you have news?"

She answers in a flat tone, "The pilot wasn't picked up. I'm sorry, Josie. I really thought this was going to be the one."

My stomach drops, and I hold the phone tighter. "Did they say why?"

"It wasn't you. You were great. There's just a lot of shows vying for audience, and the network felt there were stronger options for the lineup. But we keep going. I've got an audition lined up for you next week for a new comedy channel, and are you open to Off Broadway? There's a new show looking for unknowns who can sing."

My throat tightens, my eyes stinging with unshed tears. *Unknown.* That's me. No one knows who I am. Maybe they never will.

"Okay, sure," I manage. "Thank you for letting me know."

"Keep your chin up. Next time. It's not personal. Every no is one step closer to yes."

I nod, unable to speak for a moment. "Bye." I punch the button to end the call and slowly sink to the floor. For a moment I just stare blankly, and then I burst into tears. I really, really wanted this one. I thought for sure it was going to happen. Great script, great concept. I really nailed the character. There are so many things out of my control in this business, but it seemed like everything that could go right did. Yet it didn't.

After a good long cry, I go downstairs. I need to wallow and that means ice cream. I ignore Sean working in the kitchen. I don't want to talk to anyone right now. Instead I head straight for the door.

"Hey," he says. "You going out?"

I didn't clear it with him ahead of time, as per his request, so he wouldn't have to worry about me. So stupid. He's the most irritating guard I've ever had the misfortune to not hire. Always checking on me, never being with me.

I stop, staring at the door instead of facing him. I don't want him to see my blotchy cry face. My voice comes out in a croak. "Yeah, bye."

"Hold up."

I shake my head and walk out the door. I'm heading straight for the market for a big tub of rocky road. No, chocolate fudge. I can snarf it down faster if I don't have to chew bits of chocolate chip and marshmallow. This is an emergency ice cream moment.

"Josie."

I walk a little faster hearing Sean so close behind me. "Please leave me alone."

He catches up to me and stands in front of me on the sidewalk, blocking my path. "Wait. I haven't seen you all week." His voice softens. "What's wrong?"

My eyes sting with fresh tears at the concern in his voice. "I didn't get the pilot."

His brows draw together, his eyes sympathetic. "Are you okay?"

I can't take the sympathy in his eyes and look away. "I will be. I just need some space. You know what that's like." I laugh, but it's one of those painful kind of laughs.

"Where ya headed?"

"Don't you have a kitchen to put together?"

"It can wait."

"No, it can't. You're on a tight deadline."

I keep going down the block, practically jogging, and quickly leave him behind. I dart inside the first store I think might have ice cream. It's one of those fancy health food places, where everything's ridiculously overpriced. I can't afford this fancy ice cream, but I'm afraid any more sympathy from Sean will have me bawling in the street. I just need some time to get it together. I grab the tiniest one-serving size of what I'm sure is a quality plain chocolate ice cream and head for the counter.

Sean appears at my side, and I jump. He'd make a good ninja. "That looks like two spoonfuls."

"Yeah, well, I have to economize. I'm an out-of-work actor." *An unknown. Villager number four. No, tree number four.*

He gives my arm a tug. "Come with me. What's your favorite kind? On me. It's the least I can do after all the times you fed me and helped me out."

My lower lip wobbles, my eyes welling. "You're just feeling sorry for me."

His eyes are sympathetic, his tone soothing. "I do feel bad for you, but mostly I feel sorry for myself."

My lips part in surprise. "Why?"

"Because I missed out on seeing you this whole week, and it was my own stupid fault. I missed you."

My breath stalls, my heart thumping a little harder. He

sounds so warm and sincere. "I made myself scarce so you could get your work done."

"I know. You don't hafta do that anymore. I can work just fine with you around. You're good company."

I warm at the compliment, but then I'm suspicious. This isn't how we work. He's irritated, and I'm keeping my distance from the grump zone. "You're just being nice to me because I lost the pilot and my career is in the toilet."

"I thought we already established that I'm not nice."

"You're not. You're a jerk and a grump and completely closed off. It all adds up to one gigantic—" I wave my hands around in his direction "—irritation."

One corner of his mouth lifts. "Say what ya really feel."

I shake my head. He's really hard to stay mad at.

"Let's get your ice cream and go home."

I head to the ice-cream freezer and put my single-serving size back. "I want the most chocolatey kind."

"How's death by chocolate?"

"Great."

He pulls two pints out. "One for me, one for you."

"I could easily eat both."

"Okay, we'll get six. Is six enough?"

I laugh despite my misery. "Maybe."

He smiles. "Six death by chocolate. We'll die drowned in a puddle of chocolate goo." He gathers six pints and carries the bunch to the counter.

"It's called wallowing. Do it right, or don't bother doing it at all."

"Glad I have you to tell me the right way to wallow." He winks.

I get serious. "Thank you for the ice cream."

"Anytime."

A few minutes later, we're on our way home. Weird how I've started thinking of it as home. All I have is a suitcase, and a blanket and pillow on the floor. It's not like Sean and I are actual residents. He'll finish up soon enough. I'll have to find an apartment with a bunch of roommates and go back to waitressing, even though I suck at it. It's one of the few jobs flexible enough for me to go on auditions, which are often last minute. God, I'm so tired of getting rejected.

"How about we watch a movie tonight?" he asks. "Anything you want."

"What about the kitchen?"

"The way I figure it, I have to take the night off to save you from yourself. You'll regret six pints of ice cream in the morning."

I lift my chin. "I will never regret ice cream."

"What's your favorite movie?"

"I'm having trouble wrapping my mind around a sweet Sean."

"Desperate times, Josie. So, what is it?"

"You won't like it."

"If you like it, I'll pretend to like it. Mostly I'll watch so I can make fun of ya for liking it later."

"That sounds more like the Sean I know."

"See, I'm still in there under the layer of sweetness."

"It's an old black-and-white romantic comedy. The first one, I think. *It Happened One Night* with Clark Gable and Claudette Colbert. It's opposites attract and really funny."

"Is there a color version?"

I wince. "If there is, I don't want to see it. Look, if you can't handle a rom-com, then leave me to my wallow."

He leans close. "Okay, just between you and me, and I will deny this with my last dying breath, but the truth is, I enjoy rom-coms."

"You do?"

He laughs. "No."

I try to narrow my eyes, but they're swollen from tears, so it doesn't have much effect. "It's sublime and, if you ruin it for me, I will stab you with my spoon."

"Wouldn't a knife work better?"

"For ice cream?"

He grins. "You really are funny. I wish I'd seen you at the alternative comedy club."

"If only it was a paying gig."

We arrive home, and I unlock the door and hold it for him as he carries in my bag of ice cream.

"It's good to put yourself out there, though," he says. "Let people see what you can do. You never know who's in the audience."

"Yeah, I guess. I just do it to keep sharp."

"I'll get the spoons. Can ya pull the drop cloth off the couch? Try not to let the dust get on it."

A few minutes later, we're settled side by side, the laptop propped on boxes. Sean found the movie on a streaming service and actually bought it instead of just renting it "in case you want to watch it again later," which is so sweet it makes me mushy inside. It's his laptop, so he's kind of saying he wants me to be around and watch it again with him. I'm extra emotional right now is all. At least it makes it easier to wallow.

I dig into my ice cream in my favorite way, which is to take one thin layer at a time and work my way to the bottom. Sean digs his spoon in the center, which is the worst way to do it because it's harder in the center. He eats it in large spoonfuls.

"You're going to get brain freeze that way," I warn.

"Shh, I'm watching a sublime movie."

I snort softly and watch too. I glance over just as he presses his fingers to his forehead. "Told you."

"Shh!"

Sean finishes his pint ahead of me and actually seems to be watching the movie. I've seen this movie so many times. That's the only reason I'm watching him instead of the movie. He smiles at just the right parts. I think he actually does like rom-coms, though he tried to play it off. It's a classic and inspired so many more.

I finish my ice cream, relaxed and sleepy. I lean my head against his shoulder, and he wraps his arm around me, tucking me against his side. I could get used to this.

"I like when you're nice," I tell him.

He pauses the movie and looks down at me. "You want more ice cream?"

"No, I'm good."

"Water? Wine?"

"You have wine?"

"I could get you some. I wanna be sure you achieve a proper wallow."

I smile. "I'm good just like this."

He smiles back and presses play on the movie. I sigh in contentment. My favorite movie, a happy tummy, and a warm man holding me close. It doesn't get any better than this.

But then the movie ends. Sean takes his arm off my shoulders, putting some distance between us. I'm genuinely pissed because the moment is gone, and I want more.

"Sean," I snap, "what happened to my wallow cuddle?"

His eyes widen. "Uh, the movie ended. Are ya having a sugar crash?"

"No. I was just feeling good and now I'm not."

"Another movie?"

"Yes, please."

He hands me the laptop, and I pick another black-and-white classic, *The Philadelphia Story*, with Katharine Hepburn, Jimmy Stewart, and Cary Grant. Oh, to have been born in the heyday of Hollywood. I know the studio system wasn't perfect, but these movies are so fabulous. Witty, fast-paced banter, sexual tension, headstrong women, sophisticated men.

I lean back on the sofa and pull his arm around my shoulders. He settles me against his side and kisses the top of my head. I like that even more. I tip my face up to him in silent invitation.

"Josie." His tone holds a note of regret.

"What?"

"You're vulnerable right now."

"I'm gonna rip your head off if ya don't kiss me."

His lips curve up. "Ya sound like me."

"Good. I've been observing you closely for an authentic Brooklyn accent."

He cradles my jaw. "I heard all about my corded thick neck."

"It's a thing of beauty."

He closes the distance and presses his lips to mine for a sublime moment before pulling back, his eyes tender and locked on mine. In that moment something passes between us. He's letting me in, showing me he cares, and I feel the same. It's time. Well past time. We've been dancing around this attraction since the day we met.

Then he settles me back in place, muttering, "Watch the movie."

I do, my sad wallow giving way to a small spark of happiness. He's so warm I drift off to sleep before the movie ends.

Suddenly I'm chilled, and I realize he laid me down on the couch alone. He's standing next to it.

I reach out and snag his jeans-clad thigh. "Stay with me. I don't want to be alone tonight."

8

Josie

Sean blows out a breath, and I can tell he's about to tell me no.

"Please," I say. "I feel so much better when you hold me."

He studies me for a long moment. I must look appropriately worn out and pathetic, because he caves. "All right, come with me." He tugs me off the couch and pulls me to my feet.

I follow him. He turns off the light on this level, turns on the flashlight on his phone, and heads upstairs to his air mattress. The forbidden zone. I'm normally locked in the tower on the fourth floor on my humble floor bed. He offered to get me an air mattress, but I declined. I know it sounds strange, but it keeps me motivated to rough it, always reaching for my dream. That's how badly I want it. I'll sleep on a hard floor as a reminder that I need to persist in the face of rejection. But not tonight.

He sets his phone on the hardwood floor, plugging it into the charger, and turns to me. "Turn around."

I do. I can hear him rustling in his duffel bag, probably putting on pajamas. I'm in a T-shirt and yoga pants, which is fine for sleeping. Usually I sleep in just the T-shirt or my favorite Smokey the Bear pajamas, but I have a feeling if I go to get them, he'll change his mind about cuddling me by the time I get back. How many guys would wallow with me so wonderfully and then agree to cuddle me to sleep?

"I'm going in," I announce before diving under the comforter on his bed. The mattress doesn't bounce nearly as much as I thought it would. "It feels like a real mattress. I thought it'd be squishy like a waterbed."

I sneak a peek at him. Unfortunately, he's already in a T-shirt and gray jogging pants. No muscular display of perfection for me.

His expression is grim. "I got the quality reinforced air mattress."

"Come on over. You're part of the cuddle equation."

He rubs the back of his neck. "I'm really not a cuddler."

"Okay, then I'll cuddle you. Come on, I need your body heat. You're like a giant warm teddy bear."

He mutters something to himself.

"Don't be scared," I tease.

He picks up his phone, taps a few times, and turns it off. The room goes pitch black. His deep voice sounds gravelly. "How tired are ya?"

"Very." I say that just to get him over here. I was very tired before I considered cuddling possibilities with the man I've been secretly lusting over.

Finally, he gets under the blanket, bringing the delicious heat of his body in close range. He rolls to his side away from me, and I plaster myself against his back, wrapping my arm around his waist.

"This is lovely," I whisper. "Thank you."

"This sucks."

"Why?"

"I can't sleep with ya pressed against me like this."

"Can you just give me a few minutes of cuddle? You can put me on the floor after I fall asleep."

"I'm not gonna toss you on the floor," he grumbles, sounding like the Sean I'm used to. Somehow it's endearing now. Maybe because I know he's making an effort for me, even though he's not keen on cuddling. I'll do something nice for him tomorrow.

"Thank you," I whisper, close my eyes, and sigh in utter contentment. I stroke his chest because I'm feeling affectionate and, yes, lusty, but he grabs my hand and holds it. That's nice too.

Next thing I know, there's a loud banging in the kitchen. It's Saturday morning, and he's back to work.

I slept fantastic. He must've cuddled close all night, the sweetheart. I head upstairs, grab a fresh outfit, and take a quick shower. Today I'm going to help him in any way he needs me. He'll be working all weekend, and I will too, side by side, partners.

When I get downstairs, his back is to me in his usual T-shirt, jeans, and work boots. Sweat glistens off his rounded biceps as he hammers a length of wood molding where the wall meets the floor. A surge of raw lust nearly makes me woozy. I always knew he was gorgeous and muscled, but after the tender way he cared for me last night, I don't want him to just be my fantasy man anymore. I want him to be the real thing. Desperately.

I wait for him to pause in hammering. "Sean."

He gives me a quick glance over his shoulder, sets his hammer down, and rises to his full height of gorgeous perfection. "Hey, how're ya feeling today?"

I close the distance and wrap my arms around his neck. "Much better. Thank you for last night."

His eyes are hot on mine as his hands go to my waist, holding me lightly. "You're welcome. It was torture."

"Let me help with that." I press my lips to his in a gentle kiss that escalates quickly. He pulls me flush against him, his hands roaming all over me as his mouth devours mine. My body hums with pleasure. I moan in the back of my throat, and he breaks the kiss.

"Upstairs," he growls.

"Yes."

He grabs my hand, tugs me upstairs, and stops, standing

in the center of the mostly empty space, suddenly looking uncertain. "I'm sweaty."

"I know. I like it."

He groans and grabs me, kissing me and peeling me out of my clothes at the same time. My hands go to the edge of his T-shirt and tug. He breaks the kiss, ripping it off in a quick two-handed move. I roam my hands all over his chest like I wanted to last night. He strips me down quickly, then him, and we slam together, all grabbing hands, lips and tongue and teeth. It's wild and out of control.

His hand delves between my legs. The heel of his hand grinds against me as his fingers plunge inside me. My knees buckle, and I grip his arm for balance.

"So wet, so ready," he growls. "I've wanted you for so long."

"You were my fantasy man," I gasp out.

"You starred in all my best fantasies."

His mouth claims mine, and I'm shamelessly riding his fingers, my hips arching for more of his touch. I'm over-whelmed by him, his touch, his masculine scent, and the intensity of what he makes me feel. He cups the back of my head, his mouth shifting to my ear. "As soon as you come, I'm gonna fuck ya so hard."

I gasp, the intensity ratcheting up.

"Ya like the dirty talk," he whispers darkly in my ear and then keeps it up, bringing me ever closer to the edge. His big hand holds me by the nape of my neck while his other hand thrusts and grinds in an escalating pace that leaves me pant-ing. Oh, God. I'm so close. I open my mouth to beg him not to stop, but nothing comes out except a low keening sound, and then I explode, the pleasure rocking me helplessly against him.

"Beautiful," he croons in my ear, his hand gradually slow-ing, guiding me through wave after wave of pleasure. Finally he stills, and I cling to him weakly.

He steers me back to the mattress and lowers me onto it, spreading my legs and taking me in with gleaming eyes.

I feel too good to be self-conscious. "Condom?"

"Yeah," he croaks, tearing his gaze away.

He goes to his duffel bag and produces one. I watch him roll it on. He's thick and rock hard. I reach for him, eager to finally join with the man I've grown to admire in all the best ways.

He returns to me and settles between my legs. I expect a hard thrust, but he brushes my hair back from my face and kisses me tenderly instead. My heart hammers, a swell of emotions catching me by surprise. I've never had a guy who treated me tenderly during sex.

He guides himself in slowly, bringing a delicious ache. He groans, his eyes shutting tight. "Fuck. Ya feel so fucking good."

"You too."

He entwines our fingers together, flattening my hands on the mattress, and rolls his hips against me. I gasp as pleasure sparks through me. He keeps going with slow rolls that have my eyes rolling back in my head. I've never felt anything like it, an intense coiling tension stealing my breath with every movement. It's too much.

"Sean," I say almost desperately.

"Yeah, I know."

He kisses me, nipping my lower lip and soothing it with gentle suction, distracting me from the rapidly spiraling tightening within me as his body rocks me to ever higher levels of white-hot pleasure.

He lifts his head, his heated gaze on mine, and everything in me surges to the edge of release. My heart thuds, my breathing ragged. I need what only he can give. He rocks me on and on, his eyes never leaving mine. He releases his grip on my hands pinned to the mattress, and I grab his ass, urging him closer. He thrusts deep, holding himself still as his hand slips between us. My body jerks, and I break, the shock of pleasure radiating through me in a starburst, leaving me tingling from scalp to toes.

He surges forward, his mouth pressed to the side of my neck as he thrusts hard and deep, bringing more and more pleasure. I feel his groan vibrate against my neck as he lets go buried deep inside me.

I hold him close, catching my breath. Finally, I say, "Talk about a distraction." That's what he called me from the beginning. A distraction from his work.

He lifts his head and grins. "Best kind there is."

"You really do have a gift."

"Whatta ya mean?"

"Good in bed."

He kisses me and rolls to his side. "Takes two, darlin'."

Warmth radiates through my body, my heart dancing. I can't help my goofy smile. He called me darling.

Sean

I lie there on the mattress next to Josie, spent. It was even better than I thought it'd be. I've wanted her since we met, and the tension's been building for weeks. I held back with every ounce of control I possessed, but then she didn't get the pilot, and she really seemed to need my comfort. I'd be lying if I didn't admit part of me was glad. I didn't want to get involved with someone with one foot out the door. Now she's staying, probably for a while given the nature of auditioning, waiting, and getting rejected. I feel a little guilty that I want her to stay here in Brooklyn, but it's not like there aren't opportunities in the city for her. There's theater, and a few TV shows film there. Not as many as LA, but still. I'm not saying don't work. I'm just saying work near me.

She props up on my chest and smiles. "I feel fantastic. Endorphins at peak levels. What can I help you with today?"

I stroke her soft hair. She always means well, even if she doesn't know what she's doing. "You can take the cabinet pulls out of the boxes for me."

"And install them?"

"After I predrill the holes." No way I'm trusting her to install them. They have to be perfectly lined up.

"What else?"

"How do ya feel about weeding the garden?"

"But then I don't get to help you."

"That's a help. It needs to be done to sell the place. Hafta keep the backyard looking good."

She kisses me. "You're just trying to keep me out of your hair."

I stroke my thumb across her lower lip. "I don't want to be tempted by you all day. I won't get any work done if I'm thinking about how fast I can get inside you."

She gives me a slow sexy smile. "Tonight."

"Deal."

"Or maybe an afternoon quickie?"

I pull her on top of me and wrap my arms around her. "I wish I could stay in bed with you all day."

She presses her cheek against my chest. "Me too." Her head pops up. "But you need to get your work done. What happens when the place sells? Where will you go?"

"I'm still looking for a place, waiting for something good to open up. If I have to, I can stay with one of my brothers temporarily. Though it's not ideal. We get on each other's nerves fast if we live and work together."

She kisses me again before getting out of bed. "I'll do the garden first. I'm not sure how vital cabinet pulls are to the renovation."

"Terribly vital. No one could open a cabinet without them."

"Uh-huh." She dresses and I watch, wishing I could keep the view. She's the sexiest woman I've ever seen, all sleek toned curves. Once she's dressed, she claps twice. "Chop-chop. Get to work, boss man."

I get out of bed and grab her. She squeaks and then laughs as I spin her around. I set her back on her feet.

She beams at me, and my chest swells. All that smiling goodness aimed right at me is a powerful thing. "What a great way to start my day. Thank you."

"Thank *you*."

I get dressed again and watch as she runs upstairs.

"Garden is the other way!" I yell.

"I know! I'm changing into long sleeves and getting a hat."

I catch myself smiling for no good reason and quickly finish getting dressed. If I'm not careful, she's going to know just how much I'm into her. I don't want her to have that kind of power over me. I have to keep it light and casual until I'm sure of her.

I head back to the kitchen, whistling. I can't help but think this is a very promising start.

9

Josie

I pour my energy into weeding and, after a while, I get into it. There's something nice about digging in the dirt. And it's a comfortable sixty degrees on this late April day. Sean's right. The backyard is a big selling point because not everyone in Brooklyn has such a nice garden area. Not to mention an outdoor shower. How fun is that? My time with Sean this morning plays on repeat in my mind. Best sex of my life hands down, and I can't wait to do it all over again.

Hours later, I finish in the garden, covered in dirt and lusting for Sean something fierce.

I poke my head in the back door. "Hey, I finished."

He rises from a crouch, where he was doing something underneath the newly installed light wood island. "Excellent."

I pout a little, jutting my hip out. "I'm so dirty. I'd better not come inside." I pause. "You could though."

His eyes gleam. "I could."

"Meet you there." I lift my arm over my head and point toward the outdoor shower.

A shiver of anticipation runs through me as I reach the shower, where I got my first glimpse of a naked Sean. I let the water heat and strip down, leaving my dirty clothes on the bench. I hope Sean brings towels. I step into the warm spray and wash myself with the soap in the holder. Several minutes later, I'm starting to wonder if he changed his mind. Or maybe he didn't get my hint. Well, this sucks. Now I have to run wet and naked back to the house.

I lift my head to the sky and yell at the top of my lungs, "Sean!"

"Right here." I startle as he steps into view.

"Were you peeping at me?"

"I was letting ya get clean like a total gentleman."

"Hmmm, sounds like peeping to me. Did you bring towels?"

"Yup."

"Then get in here, you wonderful man!"

He grins and strips down, joining me. He pulls me close, kissing me, his big hands framing my face. I melt against him. There's just something so wonderful about his work-roughened hands, so competent and confident. Like him. His mouth never leaves mine as his hands stroke down my shoulders and back before sliding up my sides to cup my breasts, caressing them. My nipples tighten into peaks, and his thumbs brush across them before he pinches them. Desire unfurls in a slow wave of heat.

His gaze meets mine, and my breath quickens at the intensity of feeling I see there. I don't think I'm imagining things. He's feeling what I'm feeling, and what I'm feeling is—

I'm falling for him.

He bends to take my breast in his mouth in a tight suction that leaves me throbbing. I tunnel my fingers into his hair, holding him to me. I want to tell him I care for him, but I can't seem to form the words. I hope he knows this isn't casual for me in the least. He shifts to my other breast, his teeth gently clamping down on my nipple before sucking hard.

"Sean, I need you."

His hand presses between my legs, and then he strokes me, giving me what I need. But I need even more. He lifts his head, straightening as he searches my expression. I don't bother to hide my feelings. I want him, I need him, I care for him more than I've ever cared about any other man.

His gaze shifts away, and I feel the loss as keenly as if he'd openly rejected my feelings. He's closing himself off from me. And I know that for sure when he turns me so my back is to his front, denying me eye contact.

His hand cups my breast, the other sliding between my legs. "You're ready for me."

"More than you are," I manage, trying to give my voice an edge, but I'm too breathless. I want him to be like he was this morning, letting me in.

"Doubt it." He presses his erection against my bottom. "So ready." He strokes me in teasing circles that bring a spiraling pleasure so intense I stop thinking about anything but his fingers and the pleasure he brings me. "Spread your legs."

I do as he asks. He gives me a pinch, and I gasp. Then he steps away. I shift, watching him grab a condom, hoping to glimpse that intense look in his eyes that says he's feeling what I'm feeling.

He meets my eyes briefly before shifting his gaze to my breasts.

"Look at me," I say.

"I am," he says before shifting quickly behind me, bending me forward and thrusting inside.

My breath shudders out. With great effort, I look at him over my shoulder. His eyes are closed as he grabs my hips and thrusts deep and hard. I miss his tender gaze.

"Sweet Sean," I say because he is, and he's trying to deny it. He doesn't want me to see he has feelings for me too.

His index finger thrusts into my mouth, shocking me. His voice is gravelly, scraping against my insides. "Suck."

I do, and I'm instantly rewarded with his fingers stroking me between the legs as he thrusts slow and deep. My mind goes utterly blank as pleasure floods me in wave after wave. I'm drenched with desire, instantly on the edge of release as he takes control. There's nothing but sharp pleasure and his breath harsh in my ear. His finger leaves my mouth and pinches my nipple hard. I gasp. He shifts to cup my breast and leverages me up so my back is to his chest as he thrusts deep over and over.

His name is a chant I can't stop, my need so intense I can't manage anything more. His other hand cups me lightly between the legs, giving me soft taps in time to his thrusts, driving me insane. My release is just out of reach.

"Sean, please!"

"Please what?" he rasps.

"Give. It. To. Me."

He gives me just a little more, the pressure of his touch achingly right. His teeth clamp onto the side of my neck, and shock ripples through me just before the orgasm crashes through me. I cry out in exultation, the rush deeper than I've ever felt. He releases his hold on my neck, grabs my hips with both hands, and pounds into me. I hang onto the top of the shower wall for balance against his powerful thrusts. Shock waves of pleasure rush through me with every thrust. He lets out a guttural sound and yanks me back against him as he finally lets go.

We're both panting. I'm shaky, my legs quivering. He withdraws, and I turn to face him. His unguarded expression is fierce, possessive. He pulls me against him, enfolding me tight in his arms. That's when I realize there's more than one way for a man like Sean to show he cares. It's physical, a claiming, and I want to be claimed by him.

~

Today's my big day—a private meeting with *the* Claire Jordan. I take a few deep breaths before heading inside Luc's Bistro in the city, where I'm meeting her in a private back room. Claire Jordan! My stomach dips, nerves racing through me. I whirl and head back outside to the sidewalk. *Breathe. Breathe. Do not embarrass yourself going all fangirl over her.*

I pace the sidewalk, considering texting Sean for a reality check, but it's Saturday, which means he needs uninterrupted work time on Winnie's place. He's been such a dream all week. So tender, so sexy, so wildly, fiercely passionate. I flush hot head-to-toe remembering last night when he pinned me against the wall with his strong arms and powerful thrusts. Oh, this is bad. Now I'm lusting for Sean when I need to be focused on my Claire Jordan meeting.

Claire Jordan!

I force a slow deep breath, running my sweaty hands down my black pencil skirt. I'm wearing a white blouse too, with a pop of color in a red beaded necklace. I hope I'm not overdressed. It's just, oh, Claire was incredible in the Fierce trilogy movies and, before those, I was so inspired by her performance as a gang leader in the post-apocalyptic movie *Blue Haze*. And she's producing more awesome movies too through her production company, Red Jewel Films, some from scripts and some from books. She's putting out really original stories, and I love every movie she's ever made. Okay, I'm not going to ask her to put me in one of her movies. This isn't an ask. She's already gone out of her way, agreeing to meet me, a friend of a friend. I'm here to learn. That's it.

Professional-actress face on and go!

I stride back inside and give the maître d' my name, telling him I'm meeting Amelia Hart here, which is the name she goes by when she wants to be incognito. I heard she used to go by Jenny. Story is, that ended after she pretended to be girl-next-door Jenny for a date with a regular guy, who later became her husband. If it's online about her, I know it. She's my idol.

A scary-looking Hawaiian man with a shaved head and muscles so big they're straining the fabric of his black T-shirt appears by my side. He must be her bodyguard. "Nondisclosure," he says, handing me a paper to sign.

I glance at it and quickly sign. I would never betray Claire Jordan, but I understand her caution.

He gestures for me to follow. We go to a locked back room. He swipes a card, unlocking it, and opens the door, gesturing for me to go in. The door shuts behind me, and suddenly it's just me and *her*. The other three tables are empty, and her guard stayed outside the room.

I stare at Claire Jordan sitting at a round white tableclothed table, sipping sparkling water. Her shoulder-length blond hair is sleek, her expression composed and confident. She's in a sleeveless black and white dress, which immediately reassures me that I'm not overdressed. "Hello," she says in her throaty husky voice. "You must be Josie."

I walk forward with my hand extended. "I am. It's so nice to meet you." I take several awkward steps toward her with my hand extended, until I finally reach her to shake her hand. "I'm such a fan!"

She smiles graciously. "Thank you. I hope you don't mind I started eating bread ahead of time." She points to the bread basket. "I've got morning sickness, expecting baby number three. Keep it to yourself, okay?"

I nod vigorously and drop into my seat. "Absolutely. I signed the nondisclosure, but even without that, I swear I would never tell a soul anything we talked about. I'm just so grateful to be here. How are Owen and Harper?" I hold up a palm. "I'm not a stalker. I just research actors with careers I admire online, and the personal stuff comes up."

"Ah, okay. You're a friend of Princess Silvia's, right? Hailey spoke highly of her. Hailey's a good friend of mine."

I nod and then tell myself to stop nodding so much. "Yes. I'm dating—I'm *with*, err, I'm not sure what to call it, but Sean's her cousin. Silvia's cousin, I mean. I know Sean well. Very well." My cheeks burn. *Do not share sex stuff with Claire Jordan!* I clear my throat. "Silvia's been very gracious to me. I don't know Hailey. Your kids are adorable."

"Thank you. They're doing well. They're with my husband right now." She smiles, her hazel eyes lighting up. The effect is even more striking in person than on the big screen. "Owen's three and a half and loves playing soccer and throwing any kind of ball. He's athletic like his dad. Harper is two. I'm afraid she has my flair for the dramatic. She's quite a handful."

"They sound wonderful. You must have a wonderful family."

She smiles. "I do, thanks."

She signals toward a door in the back of the room with a

small glass window, and a waiter comes forward with menus. I take one. There's only three options, and there's no prices. I hope I can afford it.

She orders a salmon dish, and I order the warm spinach salad. How expensive could a salad be?

After the waiter leaves, she says, "I hope you're not starving yourself for a certain look. There's all kinds of shapes accepted in the industry now."

"No, I just really like salad."

"So tell me about you. How's your career going?"

I let out a breath and decide to be honest. Her career took off when she was young, but surely she'll understand how difficult it is out there. "Not as good as yours, but I'm keeping positive. I loved the Fierce trilogy and *Neighborly Attraction* and *Pleasant Town* and *Blue Haze*. Oh, there's just too many to list! I try to research actors with careers I admire, so that's how I know so much."

She leans forward. "You seem nervous. No need. I'm like you, an actress looking to make my mark. This isn't an audition. Just a conversation. I like to give back when I can, and I would've loved to have an honest conversation with an experienced actress when I was still green. Silvia mentioned you were just getting your start."

"I can't imagine you being green. You got your big break young, and now you're launched."

She takes a bite of bread and chews. "You'll find that each new level you reach has its own challenges. It's never a onetime thing, where you look around and say I'm a success. I can stop working so hard now."

"Oh."

She takes a sip of water. "But there are some things that get easier. I don't have to audition anymore. I get sent hot scripts, and I can produce my own movies and put myself in it if I want. Actually, that's something I'd recommend you do if you haven't already. Create some content and put it online. A lot of actors have gotten deals to expand their shows that way."

"I'm not much of a writer, but I could try."

"Nowadays, actors have to be a little bit of everything—actor, writer, director, producer."

"Comedian."

"Are you a comedian?"

"Yes. I mean, I do stand-up sometimes. I like comedic roles. I like all roles. I want to have my choice of genre like you and not get pigeonholed."

She nods, takes a bite of bread and chews. "Sorry for all the chewing. I need to settle my stomach."

"No problem! Completely understand."

"I was very lucky to land a movie early on that was a hit. It gave me options. It's not just about hard work. It's timing and a bit of luck."

"Yes, I totally agree. Thank you for saying that."

The waiter appears, offering small bowls of cold melon soup. "Compliments of the chef."

"Thank you," I say.

"Thanks," Claire murmurs.

I take a spoonful. "So tasty."

She takes a spoonful too. "Glad you like it. I come here a lot with my husband when we want a private meal. So tell me about your work experience so far."

I set my spoon down and consider if I should take out my headshot and résumé from my oversized purse. No, she didn't ask for it. This isn't an audition. "I was in a perfume commercial last Christmas, an educational video series about libraries, and numerous student films at NYU. I graduated from there with my BFA in drama. I've been going on auditions regularly and booked three pilots for sitcoms that weren't picked up. I'd love to work in movies. I'm a huge movie fanatic, so that's the ultimate goal."

"That's awesome. I didn't get my BFA, and I always kinda wondered if I missed out. I took classes and learned on the job. In my first movie they assigned me a personal acting coach, who I used for a while until I felt confident on my own."

"All different paths." Though I don't have to guess how she got her first breakout role. She has a look that simply shines on camera, and her voice draws attention with its throaty husky tone.

"I hope you brought your headshot and résumé."

I jolt. "Yes, I did! I didn't know if you'd want to see it." I grab my purse and unzip it, carefully taking it out, the résumé on the back of the headshot. I hand it to her. "I have a reel too you can check out on my website. It's on the résumé. Just my name. Josie Abbott."

Oh, God, I'm babbling. Chill!

She scans the résumé briefly and then takes out her phone. "I'll check out your reel right now."

My gut tightens. Why do people keep doing this in front of me? I need to stop mentioning it.

"Sure," I manage. I focus on my soup as I hear my own voice coming from her phone. I can't bear to see her expression. She could be completely unimpressed or disappointed. What if she feels like this talk was a complete waste of her time? She met with me despite having morning sickness. She totally didn't have to do that.

"I really appreciate you meeting with me," I blurt.

She holds up a finger as she watches my reel.

"Sorry." I roll the napkin in my lap this way and that, waiting for the verdict.

She smiles and tucks her phone away. "Thank God you're actually good. I was afraid I was going to have to pretend it wasn't that bad."

I beam. "Thank you so much! I'm so glad you liked it."

"How do you feel about fantasy?"

My heart races. Omigod. Is she going to offer me a part in one of her movies? "Fantasy is cool. Did you have something in mind?"

The waiter appears to clear our soup bowls. "Lunch will be here shortly."

I'm on the edge of my seat, waiting for him to leave.

Claire thanks him and turns back to me. "I bought movie rights to an epic fantasy, *Labyrinth Unraveled*."

I squeak and slap a hand over my mouth.

She smiles. "You've heard of it."

"Yes! I read young adult. I can pass for teenaged." *Labyrinth Unraveled* features a teenaged witch who finally finds a tribe like her that ultimately overturn the dystopian patriarchal society. It's basically the role of a lifetime! Huge fan base! Female-driven movie. Everything I ever dreamed of! My breath comes harder. *Do* not *hyperventilate! Ahhh!*

She goes on. "I agree, you look young. We want an unknown to play Sophie so audiences don't have any preconceived ideas tying to any previous role."

I fidget in my excitement. *Finally it pays to be an unknown!* "Makes sense," I manage to say in a calm-sounding voice.

"We're looking for eighteen and up to play her. Anyway, the book is long, so to do it justice for the fans, we'll be making two movies filmed back-to-back. We've been on a huge global search for Sophie. I mean *huge*. We looked through five thousand applications with video that we narrowed down to three hundred for screen tests, and we still haven't found the one. I'll connect you with our casting director, and you can tell her I personally vetted you, so her eyes won't glaze over. No promises, though, okay?"

"Thank you so much! This is so generous of you!"

She holds up a palm. "It's a foot in the door, nothing more. We need someone who can give Sophie some *gravitas* while also being believable as a seventeen-year-old. She's a strong empowered woman. She has grit."

"I love that! I can totally play that." I pull out my phone and drop it in my excitement. "Crap." I can't afford a replacement. I pick it up from the carpeted floor. Thankfully it's okay. "What's the casting director's number?"

She pulls out her phone and reads it to me.

I want to call right away and start prepping for the role, but then I realize that would be a take and run. "Is there anything I can do for you? Do you need a babysitter? Someone to run errands for you? Anything?"

She laughs. "I've got it covered, but thanks for offering. Few people do. Oh, and you should know we'll be filming in Vancouver for six months. Does that work for you?"

"Absolutely." My smile drops as I realize that would mean

saying goodbye to Sean. We've only been roommates for three weeks and together for a week, but I can't help but think it's the start of something significant. "When does filming start?" I laugh at myself. "She asks optimistically."

"September."

Lunch arrives, and we start eating. My mind keeps drifting back to Sean. It's early May now. If we were still together by September, we could try long distance. It's only six months. We'd only be together five months by then. Would he be willing to visit me? Would I be out of sight, out of mind?

I glance at Claire, who looks up at me and gives me a small close-lipped smile while she chews. "Is it hard on you when you're filming and you're away from your family?"

"Oh, no, my family comes with me. This business is hard on relationships. Make sure you have a partner who supports your career. My husband, Jake, traveled with me on location even before we were married. He was fully on board and worked virtually when he had to. Eventually, he went to work for my production company. Now with kids, they travel with us. Though, I'm more tired with this pregnancy and had to scale back. I've got a good team in place for Red Jewel Films, and you might've noticed I haven't taken on a major role in a couple of years."

"But *One Charmed Night* just came out at Christmas. Oh, was that filmed before?"

She wipes her mouth with a napkin. "Yeah. Sometimes they hold a film back to release at certain times of year."

I think about what she said about a supportive partner as I go back to eating. When I lost the pilot, Sean was really supportive and comforting. That's when we got together. I still. Was that a coincidence, or did he not want to be with me until he knew I wasn't going anywhere? Would he be supportive if my career did take off?

"You okay?" she asks.

I snap to attention. "Just thinking about what you said. Thanks for the advice. I think my boyfriend—I mean, we don't have an official label—but I think he'd be supportive. I don't know, though, since I haven't had something that took me away for any amount of time. Hopefully, I'll find out one day, and it'll be in a positive direction, both career and relationship-wise."

She takes a small bite of mashed potatoes, chews, and then says, "Some of my friends work it out other ways. Like, if their husband can't travel with them, they try not to be separated more than two weeks. It's a lot of flying back and forth. That takes its toll too. I suppose it's best if you just talk to your partner about it and work out whatever you think is best for you both."

"Yes, that makes a lot of sense." I try to smile but can't manage it. I've never had a guy I cared about enough to worry about this kind of thing. I'm getting ahead of myself. I don't know if I have the part in her amazing movie, and I don't know where I stand with Sean either. Though I know he cares about me. It's in his eyes and his touch, even if it's not in his words.

We finish our meal, chatting about our favorite movies, and she even shares about her kids' antics. They get really silly at bath time with bubbles. So sweet! She's surprisingly down-to-earth, and I'm just so grateful she gave me this chance.

She picks up her purse. "I need to head back, but it was great having lunch with you."

"You too! I can't thank you enough for your generosity with your time and your advice and the foot in the door. Everything! I think I'm even more of a fan now than before, which is crazy. Not insane crazy." I wince. "Sorry, I get too enthusiastic sometimes."

"Aww, you're welcome!" She stands and holds her arms out to me. I rush around the table and give her a hug.

"Thank you," I say again when I pull away.

She smiles. "The best thanks would be for you to pass it forward when you're in a position to help someone."

"I will!"

She heads out the door, looking so polished and sophisticated. I stand there for a few minutes, trying to process all the fantastic stuff that went down in this room before I realize I should go too. I grab my purse and head out, catching a glimpse of her as her guard follows by her side out the door of the building.

I wait for a moment so I don't look like I'm following her. That's when I realize she must've covered lunch for me. Claire Jordan took me to lunch! I'm totally going to pay it forward just like she told me to.

Okay, heading out now to prep for greatness! The role of a lifetime.

10

Sean

I'm exhausted, but it's all been worth it. At work we broke ground on our first Rourke Management project, with a lot of good press around it (people love that we're part of the royal family in Villroy), and here at home I'm making great progress both with the renovation and with Josie. Not that she's a project. She's a pure delight. She makes every day brighter. I love coming home to her, having dinner with her, having her in my bed. And even though I miss out on sleep sometimes because of her tempting self, I have no regrets. It's been three weeks since we got together, and what can I say? She makes me happy. I feel more like my old easygoing self again. We laugh a lot.

Today's Saturday, and I stopped working in the late afternoon to take her out to dinner. She's flying to California tomorrow for a screen test for a major movie through Claire Jordan's production company. The casting director liked the video audition she sent two weeks ago and requested a screen test at the studio. Odds are still stacked against her; there's been a lot of actresses who've done a screen test, but she remains optimistic. I'm proud of her. And she'll only be away for a week. Her agent lined up a few more auditions for her while she's there. All Josie cares about is Claire's movie.

I'm taking her someplace nice tonight. She's upstairs getting ready and told me not to peek. She wants to surprise me in her dress.

I finish getting ready and head downstairs to wait. The kitchen is really coming along. I'm estimating a week to finish. I scheduled the inspections for the following week. Somehow I did it. Winnie put a fire under my ass with her deadline, and it looks like the house will go on the market June first just like she wanted.

I signed a short-term lease for an apartment close to work, though I'm still hoping for a place in this neighborhood to open up. When I asked Josie where she was thinking of going next, she said if she had to, she could go to Nashville for a long visit with her parents, but she wasn't sure what she'd do. I don't want her so far away from me. Part of me thinks she should just move in with me. Is that too much too soon?

The doorbell chimes, and I head to the door, spotting a familiar blond head. It's Winnie here to check up on me. I'm surprised she hasn't shown up before this, considering how much she's harassed me by text.

I open the door and immediately give her an update since I've got dinner reservations I don't want to miss. "Hey, Win. Things are right on schedule. You should be able to put it on the market June first like we talked about."

She steps inside. Her blond hair is tied back in a low pony-tail, her face unusually pale. She's dressed nice, as usual, in a light green floral dress with tan sandals. "I'm sorry about the deadline. I never should've put so much pressure on you to finish quickly."

I'm momentarily speechless. I've been working night and day for weeks, and now she's sorry about the deadline?

I recover myself. "So you don't want to sell after all?"

"I don't know." Her face crumples, and she waves a hand around. "I'm sure it's great."

"What's wrong?"

Her chin quivers. "Colin and I broke up. He wanted me to get new boobs for our wedding. He was all about surface." Tears shine in her eyes, and I find it hard to sympathize over her heartbreak after the way she walked out on me to be with him. "I thought he was deep, you know? He had a real interest in art, but it was only a status symbol to him."

Does she want to move back in here? I glance behind her. No suitcase.

A tear leaks out of her eye and rolls down her cheek.

I glance upstairs, considering getting Josie down here to deal with her cousin. But then I decide to let Josie finish getting ready for our special night. I'll deal with Winnie as quickly as possible. "Sorry about Colin. What's your plan?"

She sniffles. "I told myself I wouldn't cry anymore. Let me see your good work." She wanders over to the kitchen, opening cabinets and running her finger along the teakwood-topped island. "It's beautiful."

"Thanks."

She crosses to my side. "I knew you'd do great work."

"Do ya wanna see upstairs? The bathrooms were finished since you were last here, and I repainted the upstairs bedrooms a neutral color and touched up the trim and doors."

She takes a deep shuddering breath. "I just want to say I am so sorry for the way I left you. I know it was abrupt and terribly insensitive of me. I was a fool, and I regret it."

"It's alright, Winnie. I'm fine and that was a long time ago."

Her lips press tightly together. "You're a better man than he ever was. I let him turn my head with all his lavish trips and gifts. You're the true gentleman. I never should've left you and, if it's not too late, I want to get back together."

I rub the back of my neck. I never considered getting back together with her under any circumstances. The moment she left me for another man, I cut ties. And now there's Josie. How do I explain I'm with her cousin now?

"Sean?" Winnie asks with a note of uncertainty.

"No, I don't wanna get back together."

Josie walks downstairs, looking stunning in a navy minidress with a deep V and sheer sleeves. Her red purse matches her red lipstick. A surge of affection makes me want to pull her into my arms and kiss her.

I cross to her. "You look beautiful."

"Thank you," she says, looking over my shoulder. "Hi, Winnie. I didn't know you were stopping by."

I turn back to Winnie. I can see her putting the pieces together. Josie and I dressed nice for a night out. Our familiarity. Josie's not touching me, but she stands close the way she's used to with me.

"You two are together?" Winnie asks in a small voice.

"Yes," I say.

Winnie turns narrowed eyes on Josie. "Why didn't you tell me?"

"I've been busy," Josie says. "And I'm sorry. I was going to tell you when I was sure it was going someplace."

"Is it?" Winnie asks, looking back and forth between us.

I catch Josie's eye. She gazes back at me tenderly. I can read her so well. She cares for me just like I care for her. This isn't just a convenient hookup. It's got emotion to back it up. My fingers tingle with the need to touch, my pulse quickening. This is real.

"And you!" Winnie snaps, jabbing a finger in my direction, startling me. I almost forgot she was here. "I trusted you to look out for my cousin, not seduce her!"

"I'm not a neutered monk, Winnie. Besides, she's twenty-four. Give her some credit for knowing what she wants."

"You?" Winnie asks.

"Yes."

Winnie bites her lower lip. "So you're saying it's serious?"

I glance at Josie, who looks back at me expectantly. "Yeah." I put my arm around Josie's shoulders. "It could go somewhere."

Josie's face lights up with her smile, gazing into my eyes. My heart swells. She turns to Winnie, so I do too. I hope Winnie can take the hint that there's no point in hanging around. I'm never going to be with her.

Winnie scowls at Josie. "You're supposed to be on my side, not stabbing me in the back."

Josie replies calmly, "You're engaged to another man."

I fill her in on the latest under my breath. "They broke up."

Josie inclines her head and goes on. "I know it's a little awkward—"

"A little awkward?" Winnie echoes. "It's horrible. So what, now I'm going to have to see you two sucking face every Thanksgiving and Christmas?"

Josie lifts her chin. "If you wanted him, why did you leave him in the first place?"

Winnie crosses her arms, hugging herself. "I was confused. Colin turned my head with all the lavish gifts and extravagant trips."

"Sounds like money turned your head," Josie says quietly.

Dead silence. That was harsh. True but harsh.

Winnie presses her lips together for a long moment before finally saying, "I want you both out. This is my place, and I'm moving back in."

"You can't move into a construction zone," I say. "Be reasonable."

"Did Colin kick you out?" Josie asks.

"No. He still has his apartment near work."

Josie crosses to her, putting her hand on her arm. "Let Sean finish the job. Then you can sell at a profit and buy a cute place of your own to start fresh."

Winnie bursts into tears.

"Oh, Winnie." Josie tries to put her arms around her, but Winnie jerks away and races out the door.

Josie turns back to me. "I need to make sure she's okay."

I lift a hand in acknowledgment. I expected nothing less. She told me before Winnie was like a big sister to her growing up. Still, I hope it doesn't take too long. This is supposed to be my special night with Josie. Our last night before she goes away for the first time since we met.

~

Josie

I have to run in my black pumps, which slows me down as I go after Winnie. She's racing down the block toward the park. I finally catch up when she collapses on a bench and drops her head in her hands, her shoulders heaving. Oh God. I feel terrible. I've never seen Winnie sobbing like this before.

"Winnie," I say softly, taking the seat next to her, "I love you. I never wanted to hurt you."

"Go away."

"Come on, you've always been there for me. Let me be here for you. Are you crying over Sean or Colin?"

"Both!"

"Do you want me to stop seeing Sean?"

She lifts her head. Her eyes and nose are red. "Would you?"

I hesitate before admitting the truth. "No."

"He loves you." Her voice sounds choked. "I can tell by the way he looks at you."

My heart races, my cheeks flushing. "I hope so because I'm falling for him too. I'm so sorry it didn't work out like you hoped with Colin. What happened?"

She fills me in on the man who cares more about money and status than her, and I can't say that I'm surprised. He's cool and calculating, and it was obvious those things meant a lot to him. I just hoped Winnie didn't fall into that status category. She works in an art gallery for decent pay, but she's never been rich. Maybe he saw her as someone to mold into the perfect status-symbol wife. Who requests new boobs for his bride before the wedding? Asshat.

"Win, he doesn't deserve you. That's just not right the way he treated you."

Winnie takes in a deep quivering breath. "I'm pregnant."

"Omigod! Does Colin know?"

"No." She puts a hand on her flat stomach, gazing down at it. "I just found out today. I want to keep the baby, and I've been trying to figure out what to do about Colin."

I'm not surprised she wants to keep the baby. She's thirty and was looking forward to marriage and kids. "You have to tell him."

She bites her quivering lower lip. "I'm afraid he'll try to get custody. He could afford to hire the best lawyers."

I'm thinking about lawyers and money when I realize how strange it is that she went to see Sean during this crisis. If she was here to see me, she would've let me know she was coming for a visit. And then a truly horrifying thought occurs.

I turn to her. "Did you want Sean to think it was his? Were you going to try to get back together with him and announce you were pregnant a month later? What are you doing here?" My voice gets really loud at the end, but I can't help it. Sean was the injured party in their relationship and doesn't deserve any more hurt coming his way.

"I don't know!" she cries. "The more I thought about Sean, the more I realized how much better he is than Colin. Just a better man all around. He'd be a good father."

Fury rises in me. "That's not fair to him!"

"I panicked!" Her shoulders slump, and she shifts away as if I'm a physical threat. "Please don't yell at me. I don't know what I'm doing. I'm all mixed up and hormonal and scared out of my mind."

I gentle my voice. "You can't trick Sean into being a dad."

She shifts back toward me, clutching her hands in her lap. "It doesn't matter. I asked him to get back together, and he said no. He doesn't want me. He wants you."

Damn. I can't believe she asked him to get back together while I was right upstairs. Then I remember she didn't know I was with him, and the indignation leaves me.

I take her in, she's tense and anxious, and I just feel bad for her. She lost Sean over a much worse choice in partner. I know she made her own bed with that one, but I love her, and she's in a difficult situation—pregnant, dealing with regrets and the end of the rosy future she dreamed of with Colin. "Okay, let's just keep Sean out of this picture. I'll be there for you in any way I can. One step at a time. You're going to be okay."

She nods, her eyes welling. "Thank you."

I hug her, and this time she lets me.

11

Josie

It wasn't long before Winnie called her stepmom to arrange a visit. They're close. Winnie took the subway back to her apartment to pack a bag. I texted Sean right away to let him know we're still on for dinner, and hurried home. It's our last night together before I go away for a week.

I tell Sean the deal with Winnie while we wait on the couch for our car to arrive. The restaurant is too far to walk in heels.

"Are you fucking kidding me?" he barks. "She was gonna try to trick me into being a dad to a kid that wasn't mine?"

"I'm not saying it's right. And she never could've pulled it off anyway because you don't want to be with her."

"Can ya blame me?"

"No, but in hindsight, she realized her mistake in leaving you. Haven't you ever done something you regret?"

"No."

I take his hand and give it a squeeze. "It happens."

"How can ya be so forgiving? She tried to evict us both and screw everything up."

"She's always been kind to me. I love her, and when you love someone, you cut them some slack."

He's quiet for a moment. "So I guess she's over us being together?"

"I wouldn't say completely over it, but she's got bigger fish to fry right now."

He dips his head and gives me a quick kiss. "I'm glad you dealt with her instead of me. I would've just gotten pissed."

"And rightly so. She's in good hands with her stepmom, which is probably where she should've gone in the first place. She wasn't thinking straight."

He cradles my cheek, gazing into my eyes. "You're a good person."

I smile and place my hand over his. "So are you."

He looks down at the phone in his hand. "Ride's here." He gestures for me to walk ahead of him, and locks up behind us.

After we get in the back seat, he entwines our fingers together, saying in a low voice, "I was a jerk to ya when we first met. I'm sorry about that."

"You were stressed. And I wouldn't say a jerk. You weren't nasty or anything. You were more like a big grump. It was kinda cute, like a grizzly bear with porcupine quills stuck on his butt."

He laughs. "And here I thought I was some tough badass protector for you when you just saw me as a grumpy bear."

"Grizzlies are still a force to be reckoned with if you cross them. I never crossed you. I only helped."

"You *tried* to help," he says with a smile.

"Same thing."

He rocks his head side to side. "Not exactly. Now I'm not saying it wasn't well intentioned, but sometimes you made more work for me because you don't know what you're doing."

"Well, no one said I was an expert in home renovations."

"Now that I'm looking at the end of the project, I'm actually glad you were here. You were the best kind of distraction."

"Aww, my grizzly is really a teddy bear. I knew it all along."

"Hey, none of this teddy bear stuff. I've got a rep, ya know."

I squeeze his hand. "Don't worry, I'll keep your secret love of rom-coms just between us."

"That was a joke."

"I watched you instead of the movie that night, so don't even try it. Pure enjoyment written all over your face."

One corner of his mouth lifts. "You watched me back then?"

"Yes."

"Because?"

"Because I study people to better my acting ability. Their body language, their expressions, their tones."

He nudges me with his shoulder. "You can just admit the real reason. You don't hafta make it sound like it's in service to your art."

I smile up at him. "And what's the real reason?"

He whispers right in my ear, his voice a deep rumble. "You were hot for me from the beginning."

"I totally was! But then I said no because of Winnie and because I was going away. But then I didn't go away, and you seemed to warm to me."

"Because you didn't go away." He kisses my temple and whispers in my ear, "I didn't want a hookup. That's not where I'm at."

A burst of pure happiness radiates through me, making me floaty and light. "I got that feeling."

He lifts my hand to his lips and kisses it, his blue eyes locked on mine. My heart kicks up speed as something deep passes between us. Emotion clogs my throat, the air buzzing between us. I can't resist pressing my lips to his, my fingers sliding into the soft hair at the nape of his neck.

When I pull away, he smiles warmly. I've never felt so much for anyone before, and it's overwhelming. "Sean." My voice cracks.

He nuzzles into my neck, his voice rumbling near my ear. "I've got plans for you tonight."

Part of me just wants to plaster myself against him. It's

crazy this urge I have to get closer to him all the time. But he's taking me out, so I have to restrain myself. "Can't wait."

We don't speak of anything important for the rest of the ride, but I feel different. Ensconced in a warm cocoon of love with every smile he gives me, his warm tone, his hand on mine.

He smiles and gestures out the window. "Here we are."

I look out. "It's in a hotel?"

"Yeah. Top floor with a view of the city."

"Wow," I breathe. "This looks amazing."

A short while later, I step into a large restaurant with a wall of deep red cushioned booths and an array of white tableclothed tables. It's really elegant with dim lighting from overhead recessed lights, gray walls with framed black-and-white photos, and a clear wall display case of wine. This is what I call a special-occasion place.

Sean checks in with the hostess, giving his name. We're shown to a cozy corner table right away.

After I'm seated with my napkin on my lap, I lean forward to whisper, "This place is so nice!"

He smiles, and I warm all over. "I wanted something special for you before you go."

"I'll be back in a week."

"I know, but it's the first time we'll be separated since you moved in five weeks ago."

"You keep track of how many weeks I've lived there?"

"No. I keep track of my work progress and—" He blows out a breath. "Yeah, okay, I keep track."

I bite back a smile. "You're a secret romantic, aren't you?"

He huffs. "First you call me a teddy bear and now I'm a romantic. Can we go back to when you called me an uber-talented construction worker with a corded neck, broad shoulders, and bulging biceps?"

I can't help my beaming smile. "You're the total package, I'm afraid. Embrace it."

His voice is gruff. "Josie."

"Yes?" I ask, still smiling.

"So are you."

My eyes water, my throat suddenly tight. Emotional territory, we're crossing it.

He reaches across the table for my hand, and I place my hand in his, staring at the way his large work-roughened hand envelopes mine in a warm firm grip. I think I love this man. My eyes meet his, and suddenly I know I do.

I swallow hard. Can I have a relationship with him? Will he be the kind of man who can support my career and deal with the inevitable separations? It's on my mind because I'm leaving tomorrow for a major audition for a major movie produced by my idol Claire Jordan. Claire said it was best to find a partner who supports my career, who understands the difficulty of a career that requires so much travel for long periods of time. Her husband travels with her. I can't imagine Sean doing that. He's so rooted here. He's co-owner of his family's construction business, which includes real estate development. It's not a job he could do virtually. Should I ask him what he thinks about a future with me, or will that ruin everything? Maybe he'll realize it's too difficult to be with me and end things. That would be the practical thing to do, and he's definitely a practical man.

He tilts his head. "What're ya thinking so hard about?"

The waiter arrives, breaking the moment as he takes our drink order and tells us the specials. I pull my hand from Sean's, shaken by the direction of my thoughts. I'm not going to blurt out all that deep stuff. It's too soon, and I don't want to scare him off. This must be why so many actors get together. They understand what the career demands of them. Of course, those don't always work out either because of conflicting schedules and who knows what else. It's hard enough for people to stay together when they're not separated so much.

"Josie? Where are ya?"

I snap to attention. "Sorry, my mind was wandering."

"Are ya nervous about your screen test?"

My screen test is Monday morning, and normally I'd spend the entire weekend running through the lines obsessively, a ball of anxious nerves. Instead I'm focused on Sean.

Even Winnie's situation is fading in my mind. That's bad, right? I'm already losing focus over a man. A wonderful man but still.

"I should go over my lines again," I say. "As soon as we get back."

"Maybe not first thing," he says in a low husky voice. "You did say you get an extra burst of endorphins after being with me. That can only help your performance. Hey, maybe I should go with you and give you a pre-audition orgasm."

My cheeks flush hot, and I glance around to see if anyone heard. There's no one right next to our table, so it seems it was just between us. "Would you?"

He leans back in his seat. "I was kidding. Ya know I have work. I've got one more week before inspections and—"

"I was kidding too. Can't exactly depend on you for a pre-audition boost every time. Ha-ha! What a great job that would be. Why don't they have those? Pre-audition orgasm support people. That'd really take the edge off."

"You okay?"

"Yeah, sure, fine."

The waiter returns and pours a small amount of merlot for us both to taste from the bottle we ordered. After the wine is poured, Sean raises his glass to mine. "To a fantastic screen test. I know you'll do great."

I clink my glass to his. "To a winning screen test." I sip right away because I'm just superstitious enough to believe it's necessary after putting my wish out into the world.

I take a deep breath and blurt, "You know if I do have a winning screen test, it means I would be in Vancouver for six months."

"We'll cross that bridge when we come to it. For now let's enjoy the moment."

He sounds so confident and sure that I relax. He said *we'll* cross that bridge, which means we'll work out something mutually agreeable. I think. I'm new at this relationship stuff. I've never felt like this before, never truly been in love before. What I had with my college boyfriend was nothing like the intensity of what I have with Sean.

I let it go. I'm good at enjoying the moment and that's exactly what I'll do. "This moment sitting here at an elegant restaurant with my sexy gorgeous…" I wait for him to fill in the blank. *Boyfriend, say boyfriend.* It's officially a relationship, right?

"Man. The word is man. Do *not* say teddy bear."

"My sexy gorgeous manfriend."

He laughs. "Were you checking if you could call me your boyfriend? Go ahead. I already think of you as my girlfriend."

A warm glow fills me up to bursting. "Dinner with my sexy gorgeous boyfriend is the moment I'm in, and there's nothing better than that."

He leans forward and whispers, "Except for what comes after." He winks. "You."

I lean close. "Now you're going to make me think about sex all through dinner."

He smirks. "Good. Mission accomplished."

Dinner goes by in a sparkling blur of delicious food, wine, and sexy man. At least from my side of the table. I'm relaxed and full of affection for my guy.

The moment we leave the restaurant, I hug him. He wraps an arm around me. "What's this hug for?" he asks with a note of surprise.

"I'm just happy." I give him a squeeze before pulling away.

He takes my hand and walks with me toward the elevator. The moment the doors close, he pins me against the wall and kisses me breathless.

He breaks the kiss, his eyes gleaming as he pulls me flush against him. "I got us a room."

"Really?"

He holds my jaw, his words running hot over my ear. "I wanted to have you in a real bed not on an air mattress."

"But I need to catch a flight tomorrow morning. I didn't…" I trail off as his hand slides down my spine in a hot trail before landing on my ass. My breath catches. "I didn't bring an overnight bag."

He gives me a squeeze. "We're not gonna sleep here. It's just for total Josie debauchery."

He's so romantic! I grab his head and pull him down for a kiss. "Yes! Thank you."

He grins. "For a minute there I thought you weren't on board."

"I'm always on board for debauchery. What exactly does that mean?"

"It means I get to take my time with you. I get to make you scream my name. I get to make you forget every other man you've ever been with."

"You already accomplished that last part."

He presses his forehead to mine. "Josie." His voice is tender, and so is his kiss. I'm falling in love for the first time, and I can't worry about the future. Now is glorious. It's like a little ball of sunshine lighting me up inside. Magnificent.

～

The hotel door shuts behind me, and I wander in to check out the king-size bed with a fluffy white down comforter. I turn to Sean. "Looks comf…" My voice trails off. There's something predatory in his eyes as he unbuttons his shirt, slowly approaching the bed.

Goose bumps break out over my skin. "Sean?"

"Take off your dress."

I flush hot at the commanding tone, but I'm just uneasy enough to hesitate. He pulls his shirt off and tosses it over the back of a chair before closing the distance between us. His arms wrap around me, his fingers trailing up my spine to the zipper of my dress.

"Need some assistance?" he asks, the words hot against my ear. He doesn't wait for my reply, simply unzips it, and pulls it off me. He tosses it to the chair and pulls me against him, his lips meeting mine in a hungry kiss.

My limbs go weak, and I melt against him, sliding my hands under his undershirt, stroking the muscular heat of his back. His nimble fingers make quick work of my bra, tossing it before his hands caress my breasts. I close my eyes. He makes me feel so good, so relaxed and languid. I don't know why he seemed predatory—

"Ah!" I land on the bed with a bounce. He just tossed me here.

He climbs over me with a grin. "Couldn't wait." He pulls my panties down and off. Then he shifts me, sliding the blanket out from under me and somehow managing to brush his stubbled cheek against my nipples at the same time. They dutifully come to attention.

"How come I'm the only one naked here?" I ask with a mock pout.

"Because it's Josie debauchery night."

He kisses me, giving my lower lip a nip. I wrap my arms around him, but I can't hold him for long as he kisses and tastes his way down my body, lingering on my breasts, which he sucks and bites, jolting me before moving down, down, down. My stomach tightens in anticipation.

His big hands spread my legs as he shifts, settling between them and placing a gentle kiss on my sex. He shifts my legs over his shoulders, pushing me open wider. His gaze meets mine, both tender and possessive, and every part of me reaches out to that part of him. I want to be his. I want his tender love. There's no question in my mind that's what he's offering.

"Sean," I murmur with all the warm affection that's coursing through me in this moment.

"Josie," he returns with equal warmth. "Watch." He dips his head and laps at me.

My head falls back on the pillow, a sound escaping that's half moan, half gasp. And then my hips arch at the intense sensation. His mouth is incredible. Wicked. All consuming. I could sing its praises in endless tribute to the highest mountaintop. And then his finger slides inside me and another. I grip the sheets as my world takes a dizzying spin of pleasure, my insides coiling tight and hot.

"Oh my God," I gasp out. "Don't stop."

He doubles the intensity at my words, and I'm left panting, unable to speak, my hips rocking of their own accord, riding his fingers and mouth shamelessly. The room goes dim, everything narrowing down to the intense edge that he's pushing me to relentlessly. Oh God, I'm so close.

And then it hits me in a lightning jolt of pleasure, my entire body arching off the mattress as I cry out in pure exultation. A rush of pleasure rocks me on and on. He gentles, letting me ride out the aftershocks of a pleasure that never seems to end. Finally, he eases off, leaving me limp and languid.

I cup his head, running my fingers through his soft hair. "Sean, you wonderful man, fuck me."

He nuzzles my inner thigh before lifting his head. "I want you so bad."

I lift my arms to him then drop them weakly to the mattress as he climbs out of bed and quickly strips down. He had a condom in his pocket, which he wastes no time rolling on.

Then he's on me, pushing slowly inside, his face over mine, his blue eyes smoldering with an intensity that steals my breath. He moves slowly, deliberately, each thrust bringing another wave of sensation. His hand slides under my hip, tipping me up for his next deep thrust. My head arches back at the intense sensation of him filling me to the hilt.

"Feel so good," he says hoarsely, his big hand cradling my jaw.

"You too," I say on a gasp as he thrusts again.

Our eyes lock as we share a breath and then another, his thrusts rocking me, higher and higher. Time stops and there's nothing but this—our intense connection, our passion, our love.

I explode with a sharp cry, the orgasm sneaking up on me, going on and on as he thrusts hard and fast. Suddenly, his head arches back, the cords of his neck pulled tight, and he lets go with a guttural groan, collapsing on top of me.

My sweet Sean. I hug him, and he nuzzles into my neck, murmuring something that sounds like praise.

I can't make out his words, but it doesn't matter. Deep down, I know. He cares for me just as deeply as I do for him. I love him. And I think he loves me too. Tears prick my eyes at the overwhelming feelings coursing through me. It finally happened for me with the most wonderful man in the world. I never want this feeling to end.

But how can I hold onto it, to him, with our diverging paths?

~

Sean

I close my eyes, euphoric and relaxed. I hear a sniffling sound and look over to find Josie wiping tears. I prop up on an elbow, alarmed. "Why're ya crying?"

"I'm just happy."

My brows scrunch together. She never cries after sex. "What's going on? Did Winnie say something about me?"

"Nothing bad. Don't worry. I just felt so happy it sort of bubbled over into a few happy tears." She climbs out of bed. "This was amazing. Let's get back though. I need to run my lines."

I watch as she dresses quickly, still feeling like something is off.

"Come on," she urges, taking my hand and trying to pull me out of bed.

I help her out and roll out of bed on my own. "Sure you're okay?"

"Yes!"

I'm not convinced, but I let it go. She's got a lot going on with all that's riding on this audition. Not to mention Winnie barging in right before I whisked Josie away to dinner and hotel-room sex. It's a lot for one night.

The moment we get home, she says, "Thanks for the endorphin boost," gives me a kiss, and races up to her fourth-floor room.

I settle on the couch to wait for her. Our days here are numbered. I don't want to stop living with her. I'm going for it. I don't care if it's fast. When she gets back from her trip, I'm going to take her to see my new apartment and invite her to move in. I think about what I'll say. I want her to know we have a real future together. We get along so well, and we already live together.

I scrub a hand over my face. That's dancing around the truth. The fact is, I've fallen for her. I've done everything in my power to resist her, but it was an impossible task and, once I stopped fighting temptation, it was easy to love her. She's amazing. A beautiful person inside and out.

It gets late, and I go up to see if she's done rehearsing yet. She's asleep on the floor, script pages under her cheek. My Josie, uber-talented actress. I want her to get her big break and, at the same time, I don't. I want her to be happy with me here.

I scoop her up and carry her downstairs to my bed, carefully setting her down. She lifts her head, murmurs, "Night," and goes right back to sleep.

I settle in behind her and spoon her, stroking her hair. Suddenly I don't want her to go. It's just a week, but it feels like more. What if she doesn't come back? What if she crashes on a friend's couch out there and goes on even more auditions there instead of here? My arm tightens around her waist. Now that I finally let her in close, I'm having trouble letting go. Like she's leaving me for good. It's just traveling for work. She'll be back.

Odds are, she'll be back.

12

Sean

I did it. It's Saturday night, and I finished the renovation an hour ago. Inspector will be here Monday morning. I'm exhausted, and it's not from work either. It's because Josie still isn't back, and I'm having trouble sleeping without her. I even tried spooning her pillow, but it's no use. I can't believe I got used to her so much that I can't sleep without her. Eventually I fall asleep, but it's not until I black out around three a.m. Insomnia sucks.

At least it's for a good reason. Josie did so well on her screen test they asked her to extend her stay. There's a callback audition on Monday with a short list of five candidates for the lead role. Still not great odds, and I feel guilty for being glad for it. I know that's wrong. If you love someone, you should set them free when they need to be free. Only it feels like shit. What if she gets it? She'll be thousands of miles away in Vancouver for six months. That is not a short flight either. We should cut ties before then. It'll be too painful to drag it out. Long distance never works out. She'll meet some hot idiot on set and forget all about the construction worker she once knew in Brooklyn.

My phone vibrates, and I pull it from my pocket. It's my

younger brother Jack. *Hey, I need a wingman tonight. Sam's too pussy whipped to go out.*

Jack's best friend Sam recently got engaged and basically ditched his guy friends in favor of his fiancée. Lame.

I text back. *Sure. Where?*

Tazi.

I'm in. That's a bar in Williamsburg, a happening neighborhood, where they serve up beer in giant chalices.

Cool. Meet me there.

Jack lives in Williamsburg, so he'll probably be on his second beer before I get there. Subway trip's about a half hour or so.

When I get there, the place is crowded. The bar has a dive feel to it in a cool way—exposed brick, copper ceilings, and a long black-painted brick wraparound bar with black and red vinyl seats. There's a pool table in back I hope we'll play. Jukebox is playing Judas Priest, and there's a noisy crowd out on the patio. I text Jack that I'm here.

Jack: *At the bar.*

I spot him around the corner of the bar, and he gestures me over to where he's flirting with two pretty brunettes. Ah, hell. Was this a setup? Leave it to Jack. He could've told me. I thought he just wanted a wingman while he cruised the bar.

His dark brown hair is neatly parted on the side, longish on top in a tousled look that definitely took some product to achieve. He's got a neatly trimmed beard going on too, dressed casually in a white V-neck T-shirt and faded jeans. He flashes a smile at my arrival and slaps me on the back before turning to the ladies. "This is my brother Sean. Sean, this is Sherry and…sorry, I forgot your name."

"Jane," she says drily, the silver stud piercing on her tongue catching the light. I'm not into piercings. "I know, such a tough name to remember."

"Get to know Jane," Jack says to me before turning to Sherry.

Jane huffs, Sherry giggles, and I grit my teeth. I clap a hand on Jack's shoulder and take in both women. "Nice meeting you both. Jack and I are gonna play pool now. Have a good night."

I incline my head for him to follow, not bothering to wait. The pool table has a game going, so I lean against the wall, watching. Jack appears at my side a few minutes later with a chalice of beer in each hand. The women have already moved on to flirt with a couple of guys farther down the bar. Saturday night bar cruise. I don't miss it.

Jack hands me a beer. "I forgot you were still burnt from you-know-who." He takes a long swallow of beer, already over anything he might've had going with Sherry at the bar. "Ya really need to get back out there." I debate telling him Josie and I are now a thing. He's notorious for pulling pranks, so I'm cautious what I give him for ammunition.

"I don't like being set up."

He gives me a sideways look. "You work day and night. No woman for almost a year now. No wonder you're cranky."

"I'm not cranky," I snap.

"Right."

"I'm cranky right now because you set me up."

"I didn't. Those girls started talking to me, and I just included you. I didn't ask ya to come here for that." He takes a sip of beer and turns back to the bar. Sherry blows him a kiss over the shoulder of another guy. He winks and turns back to me. "Forgotten already."

I snort. "Easy come, easy go."

"Always."

The game ends, and I'm about to ask if we can join the next game when the three guys move on. Jack and I get our cues from the wall rack.

"Let's make it interesting," he says, pulling a coin from his pocket. "I'll give you this ancient Roman coin worth five large if you win. If I win, I get five hundred cash. How 'bout it?"

"Yeah, right. Does your ancient Roman coin squirt water?"

"No."

"Electric shock? Leak ink?"

He flips it through his fingers, weaving it in and out. "Have I ever steered ya wrong?"

"Ya think I'm an idiot?"

"Geez. One prank, and you're forever branded as untrustworthy."

"More than one. Excuse me if I'm suspicious that you're walking around with a rare five-thousand-dollar Roman coin in your pocket."

He flips it in the air. "Your loss. It's from the Italy of the desert."

I set up the balls and break. "What're ya talking about?"

"The Bellagio, or was it the Palazzo? It was an Italian name."

"Vegas?"

He sets up for his shot. "Where else?"

I shake my head, laughing.

He straightens. "Hey, I just remembered you have a woman roommate. Is she the reason you're not into the bar scene?" He studies me for a moment. "Still pretty cranky, though. I'd wager ya didn't close the deal."

"I'm only cranky because I haven't been sleeping well."

"Because you're tossing and turning, wishing you could get with her? I'll tell ya right now, never hook up with the roommate. The moment things end, you're in a living hell. Suddenly, there she is in the kitchen, in the living room, all up in your space. Really bad move. Happened to a buddy of mine."

I shake my head, take a sip of beer, and set up for my next shot. "She's a temporary roommate anyway." *And I want her to be permanent.* I keep that to myself because I'm starting to realize a future with Josie isn't at all a sure thing.

"So you did get with her. Then why're ya so cranky?"

It's still my turn, so I set up for the next shot. "Ya talk too much."

"Text her and tell her to meet up with us. I wanna meet her."

I exhale sharply. "She's in LA for a callback audition for a major movie."

"Cool."

"I guess."

"You guess?"

I miss the shot by a mile. "If she gets it, she'll be away for six months."

"And?"

I don't bother to answer, focusing on my beer. I know it's wrong to want her to stay, but I can't help it. Why did I let myself get close? I knew it would always come to this. My place is here. Hers is all over the world—LA, Vancouver, wherever else they film stuff. What the hell am I doing with someone like that? I knew better, but I couldn't seem to help myself. I rub my temple at the headache forming there.

Jack makes his next shot and turns to me, a knowing look in his eyes. "Ya fell for her, didn't ya? I give ya credit for getting back on the horse. Sure, I wouldn't have gone for my ex's cousin slash roommate slash future movie star, but ya never did have much sense when it comes to women."

I bristle. "What's that supposed to mean?"

He cocks his head. "It means ya fall hard, and it's not always for someone in your league."

"Bullshit."

"Bro, Winnie was high class, all uppity, calling you gentleman all the time, taking you shopping for a new wardrobe. Hell, she made ya think you belonged in that ritzy neighborhood. You don't. That's for the money. She left you for money too. An actress about to make a major movie is not in your league either. You're always reaching above yourself, and you're never gonna be satisfied that way. Just sayin'."

"Fuck you. I'm not confined by my circumstances."

He shakes his head. "Look around. This is the kind of place we belong. Not a fancy art gallery, a money neighborhood, or mixing with the Hollywood set."

He takes his next shot and misses. A sick sense of victory goes through me. Jack is wrong about where we belong.

I cross to his side and lower my voice. "Didja forget we're royalty? We could be living in a kingdom if we wanted."

He barks out a laugh. "Be serious. We're the riffraff of the family. I don't care if Dad's happy to visit his kingdom now as an honorary grandfather. That's not us."

I pick my next shot and take it. "I'm ambitious, and I make no apologies for that, but that doesn't carry over to relationships. I'm not a social climber."

He arches his brows. "It's a relationship, huh?"

I set my jaw. "Yes." Though I'm having serious doubts about it now. I couldn't seem to resist her. I tried. Is Jack right about me having no sense when it comes to women? Is that why it never works out?

He jabs a finger at me. "You're what we call in the biz a serial monogamist."

"So?"

He shakes his head. "So that's a tough way of life. You fall, you crash, you fall, you crash."

I set up my next shot, determined to win this game. Jack's irritating the hell out of me, mostly because I'm starting to think he's right. I fall and I crash, over and over again.

I straighten. "And what do you do? Hook up, leave, hook up, leave."

He takes a long swallow of beer. "I never fall. It's all fun all the time."

"Maybe you're the one who's missing out," I snap. "Look at Dylan with Ariana. Have ya ever seen him so happy?"

He lifts a palm. "Hey, take it down a notch. I'm not trying to piss you off."

I take the next shot. At least I'm doing well at pool. "I'm just tired. All work no play this week."

"I'll let you win at pool."

"Ha! Ya never let me win. I'm just more skilled."

He chuckles.

I do win, and Jack flips me his Vegas coin. I catch it and it bends in my grip. It's made of soft rubber.

He laughs. "Superstrong man, ya broke it. Don't ever want that to happen."

Then I realize it's soft because it's actually a condom in coin packaging. I pelt him in the head with it.

He laughs. "It really is from Vegas."

Josie

I've been in LA for a week and a half now, which is both good and bad. It's good because the casting director asked me to stick around for a callback audition, and bad because I miss Sean so much more than I thought I would. We've been in touch by text and a few short phone calls since he's so busy with work. Fortunately, he finished the renovation on time, and inspections went smoothly. It's looking like he'll be moving out this Friday. I'm not sure where I'll land. I don't want to assume he wants me to live with him at his new place. Winnie's still at her dad and stepmom's house. It's looking like a visit to my parents before I regroup once again for waitressing and auditions.

Maybe it won't come to that. I'm supposed to hear from my agent today if I booked the movie. I felt my callback audition was solid. I met the director, cried on cue (twice), and changed up my take on the scene at her direction. There's five of us going for the role. I haven't met the others and, since they're unknowns, I don't know what my competition is like.

Now I'm on my way to the airport in a car paid for by the studio on this sunny Wednesday morning, heading back home. Funny how I think of Brooklyn as home now. Maybe it's Sean I think of as home. I've always moved around a lot and never really felt like I had a home before. It's only six a.m., too early to hear back, but I check my phone anyway. Nothing. I really, really want this role. Sophie is everything I've been looking for in a role—a strong empowered woman, who has her own adventure saving the world. It's such a rarity to find this kind of script, and the complexity of her character will be an ideal showcase for my acting range. It's a springboard to more work. I'm sure the movie will be commercially successful. It already has a huge fan base from the book. Gah! It's so hard to wait.

I watch a movie on the flight home and then just listen to music. I powered down my phone for the flight, and I'm hoping when we land, I'll turn it on and get the news I've been dying to hear.

We land and I power on the phone with shaking fingers, my heart in my throat.

No news.

I remind myself that I might be in a hurry to find out, but that doesn't mean the studio is. No news is good news. They're still considering. Maybe it's really close between me and one other actress, and they're debating between us.

Still no news as I take the AirTrain and then the subway. It's now five p.m. New York time, which means it's only two p.m. in LA. I tell myself I'll hear by the end of the day LA time. I'm no longer on edge at this point. I can only stay worked up for so long. I'm looking forward to seeing my grandmother's old brownstone now that Sean finished the renovation. We have only tonight to enjoy it in its finished state before we have to move out tomorrow night.

I step out onto the sidewalk on a warm sunny spring day. It's late May, birds are singing, daffodils blooming, and people I pass on the street seem to look a little brighter. My phone vibrates, and I whip it out of my back jeans pocket. It's my agent, Jade.

Adrenaline pours through me. I answer with a trembling finger to accept the call. "Hi, Jade." I stand frozen on the side-walk, waiting to hear my fate.

"Josie, it was close. They really liked you, but they wanted someone with a more exotic feel that would play well internationally."

"Is it my hair? I can dye it."

"They chose an actress from Venezuela. They liked the cadence to her English."

"I can do accents. Did you tell them that? I can work with a dialect coach."

"Not this time. Keep your chin up. You're close. And remember that just because you didn't get it, you're still up one. You met and auditioned for a casting director for a well-respected production company. She'll remember you and maybe recommend you for another project down the road."

I blink back tears, my throat tight. I know that, of course. I'm just tired of being close, but never grabbing the prize.

"I feel like I'm never going to break in," I whisper.

"You will. Would I keep sending you on auditions if I didn't believe in you? Hell no. I'd drop you like a hot potato. I only stick with clients I believe are going somewhere. It's just a matter of the right project at the right time. You've got the stuff. You just keep doing your thing, I'll do my thing, and one day we'll be toasting your success. Don't forget to thank me at the Oscars."

A tear escapes. "Yeah."

"I'll be in touch."

"Thanks, Jade."

"You got it. Talk soon."

She hangs up, and I have the sudden urge to throw my phone. I restrain myself and trudge down the sidewalk. Sean won't be home yet. He said he'd be here around six. I'm actually glad because now I can have a good cry in privacy.

Which I do.

Then I curl up on the couch and watch *It Happened One Night*. Sean gifted it to me before I left so I'd have my fave movie while traveling. I'm so glad. This movie always makes me smile.

Sean gets home halfway through the movie and strides toward me, a big smile on his face. "You're back!"

I hit pause on the movie and stand. "I'm back." I'm glad to see him, but I can't seem to manage a smile in my dark mood.

He pulls me in for a tight hug and kisses the top of my head. "I missed you."

I hug him back, the lump in my throat back in full force. "I missed you too."

He loosens his hold and cups my jaw. "What's wrong?"

"I didn't get it." My eyes well, my throat tight. "My agent told me they wanted someone more exotic. They went with an actress from Venezuela because they liked the cadence to her English."

"Sorry." He strokes my hair. "I know you really wanted it."

I pull away, swiping an errant tear with my knuckle. "I feel like it's never going to happen for me. Am I just wasting my time? I keep up with classes, I audition all the time, and all I have to show for it is a commercial and an educational video series nobody cares about."

"It's a tough career."

I start pacing. "I know. I knew that going in, but how many times am I going to get close and then get passed over? I still love acting, but nobody will let me do it."

"Maybe you could create your own project to be in."

I throw my hands up. "I've done that. I've done tons of student films too. It's not the same. I want something that people will actually see."

He takes a seat on the couch. "What can I do for you? Is this an ice-cream-wallowing situation? You wanna go out for dinner?"

I flop down next to him. "I'm too miserable to be hungry."

He wraps an arm around my shoulders. "Maybe you could stay local, audition for stuff here in New York. There's lots of theater, and a few TV shows film here." He sounds upbeat about the prospect, which only makes me feel worse.

I grip my hands tightly together. "I feel like you don't get how upset I am right now."

"I get it. I'm trying to make ya feel better. You chose a tough career. I'd like you to lean on me, let me be your foundation." He cups the side of my face, turning me toward him. "Move in with me at my new place. I'll take care of you, and you'll never have to worry where you're gonna crash next."

I go cold. "Take care of me?"

"Yeah. I'll be the breadwinner, and you can have a home, finally put down roots. You always said you never had a real home. I'll give you one."

I push his hand away and scoot back. "It sounds like you don't think I'll ever support myself."

He opens his mouth and shuts it again.

I speak through my teeth. "What?"

"Okay, but do that while you're with me. Here in Brooklyn."

I take a slow deep breath. I'm getting a very bad feeling about where Sean stands on my career. "I'm going to keep auditioning. It could be my very next audition that's my breakout, and then I could end up far away, filming. Would you be okay with that? Would you travel with me, or visit me regularly?"

"I'm pretty rooted here with my job and all, but I'm sure I could squeeze in a visit. Realistically though—"

"Realistically?" My voice comes out high and reedy. I force a level tone. "Am I living in a fantasy world thinking I can make it as an actress?"

He puts up a palm. "All I'm saying is I don't want ya to worry. I have a good job, so let me take care of you."

Something in his tone rankles. It's not flattering what he's offering. It's insulting. "How do you see our future?"

"I'll give you a good foundation, like I said. I'll keep building Rourke Management. We'll get a nice place together in a nice neighborhood. Maybe we'll get a dog. I'll introduce ya to my family. We'll build a life here, and you'll never have to worry about where you're gonna crash next, or if you can afford ice cream or whatever. You won't have to worry about a thing here with me."

I can't help but notice he didn't mention my career at all. He assumes without him my life will always be like it is now —a struggling actress forced to be frugal, crashing on people's couches. He doesn't believe in me. A cold quiet anger settles over me. Claire Jordan's wise advice runs through my head: *Make sure you have a partner who supports your career.*

I stand. "I don't want you to take care of me. I'm at a low point right now, and I've got nowhere to go but up. And I'll do that through my own grit and perseverance. Not because I depended on a man to take care of me."

He blows out a breath. "Josie, I'm not being sexist. I love you."

My eyes widen. That's the first time he said that. But his love comes with one big condition—be his little pet tucked away safely—and I can't accept it. "No."

"I don't love you?"

I swallow hard. "When you love someone, you support them in what they care about the most."

"I do support you. That's what this is all about."

I attempt to explain. "Like Claire Jordan's husband traveled with her even when they were just dating, and he works for her now. They're never separated for her work because he's fully on board."

He shakes his head. "You don't even have a job. How is this a thing? You want me to travel with you to a job that doesn't even exist? I should quit my job because you *might* get something in a year? Or five?"

I turn away, equal parts hurt and angry. I'm having serious doubts about Sean, and I don't know if it's because of what he's saying, or if I'm just reeling from this audition rejection. It really feels like he doesn't believe in me, like he always thinks I'll be hopelessly spinning my wheels, and he has to rescue me from myself. I wish I knew. All I know for sure is everything feels wrong right now.

"I need to take a step back." I grab my laptop and shove it in my purse. "I'm going to Winnie's place in the city." I head for the door, snagging my wheeled suitcase.

"When will ya be back?"

"I don't know." My voice cracks. "I just need to figure some things out."

I walk out, and he doesn't follow me. I can't be with someone who doesn't believe in me when there's already so many people telling me no. I need to surround myself with supportive people. It's the only way for me to survive.

I make my way to the subway through a blur of tears.

13

———

Josie

By the time I get to Winnie's apartment building in the city, my eyes are swollen from crying too much. Then I remember she's still at her dad and stepmom's house and let out a stream of curses. Now what? I don't want to crash at a friend's place with my eyes so red and swollen. I'm sure I look a mess, and who wants that showing up on their doorstep?

I pull out my phone and call Winnie. "Hi, it's me. How're you?"

"What happened? You sound upset."

I blink rapidly, trying to hold the tears at bay. "I'm at your apartment in the city and my life sucks and I just wanted a place to crash. I'm such an idiot. I forgot you weren't here."

"I am. I'll be down in a minute."

I nearly collapse with relief. I tuck my phone away and step into the lobby. I hope the fact that she's home means she's doing better. She's got much bigger things to deal with than I do. Here I am crying over an audition rejection and an unsupportive boyfriend when she's dealing with a pregnancy with her asshole ex.

She appears in the lobby a few minutes later, her expression sympathetic. "Come on, we can lean on each other during this sucky time."

"I'm sorry to bother you. I know you're dealing with some heavy stuff."

"We'll talk upstairs."

I nod and follow her to the elevator. Once we're inside her apartment, a nice one-bedroom furnished mostly with white furniture with touches of glass and chrome in the end tables and coffee table, she pours us each a glass of white wine and takes a seat on her couch, patting the spot next to her. Soft classical music plays in the background. Winnie is so cultured and sophisticated. It was something she aspired to and achieved beautifully. She might be a little dreamy, but she's living the life she always wanted, so maybe that's not such a bad thing.

I take the offered seat. The couch is too firm to be comfortable. Probably Colin picked out everything to his taste. But couch crashers can't be picky.

"So what's sucky for you?" she asks.

"You first. I'm sure yours is much suckier."

She lets out a shaky breath. "Okay, well, I miscarried."

"Oh, Winnie! I'm so sorry!" I should've noticed she poured herself a glass of wine, which she wouldn't do if she was pregnant.

She nods, quiet for a moment. "Thanks. I cried for three days straight, and then I seemed to be out of tears. So here I am."

"Did Colin know about the pregnancy?"

"No. I was going to meet him in person last Saturday to tell him, but I miscarried the day before. How's that for timing?"

"I'm so sorry." I hug her.

She pulls back and sighs. "It wasn't meant to be."

She takes a long swallow of wine. I do the same.

I'm sure Colin won't let her stay here for long. He paid for it. "Are you looking for a new place?"

"I'm moving back to my place in Brooklyn until it sells. Then I'll use the money to buy into a co-op here in the city. I want to be close to work. New York is the center of the art world. At least that's what my boss always says." She gives me a small smile.

I smile back. "That sounds like a good plan."

"Now you."

"It's nothing."

"Jo-Jo, I have known you your entire life. Do *not* come in here with your red swollen eyes and blotchy face and tell me it's nothing."

"Jo-Jo," I echo softly. "Haven't heard that one in a while." My family called me that until I was a teen when I insisted they call me the more sophisticated Josie. Funny how I thought that was sophisticated back then when my full name is much more so, Josephine.

I sigh and take another sip of wine. I can feel her eyes on me. I know she won't judge, but I'm afraid if I say it out loud, I'll start crying again. My eyes hurt too much to cry anymore.

She elbows me. "I'll sit here quietly waiting for you to spill, until this entire bottle of wine is empty if that's what it takes."

I drain my glass, about to tell her my career is in the toilet. Again. But what comes out is, "Sean and I argued about something pretty important to me, and I think it's a relation-ship ender. I'm not sure. I'm really confused."

"Can you be a little more specific?"

Now why did I start with that? My sob story started with my crappy rejection today. Another close, but no thanks. Not exotic enough! What the hell do they want from me? If I'd known they wanted an accent, I would've done one. I can pick up any accent easily thanks to my nomadic childhood.

I fill her in. "I was up for the lead in what is definitely going to be a major movie, and I didn't get it because I'm not exotic enough."

She gives my arm a squeeze. "I'm sorry. Why did you and Sean argue? It wasn't because of me, was it? I'm okay with you guys being together."

"No, it wasn't because of you. It was because he doesn't believe in me. I've got enough people not believing in my abilities, thank you very much." My voice cracks, completely ruining my attempt to sound indignant. "I hate feeling like this, like I can't stop crying." I knuckle away more tears. "I don't know if I'm more upset about the audition or Sean."

She lifts the wine bottle and pours me more wine. "I'm sorry you didn't get the part you wanted, but you always bounce back from that. I've never seen you fall apart over an audition. Tell me what happened with Sean."

I take another long swallow of wine and lean back into the couch, looking at the ceiling and willing my tears back. "This couch is so uncomfortable."

"I know. Colin picked it for the lines. Hold on." She transfers her wineglass and the bottle to an end table, pushes the coffee table out of the way, and takes a seat on the floor on a thick white shag rug with a swirling pattern.

I join her with my wineglass, and we lean back against the couch. "Much better."

"Did Sean say he doesn't believe in you? That doesn't sound like something he'd say. He's never deliberately hurtful."

I study her for a moment. "Are you still in love with him?"

She gives me a rueful smile. "No. I think I was just looking back with nostalgia to him in my desperation for a better future for me and the baby. Sean felt safe. It goes back to his natural protectiveness."

I think about how safe I felt with him right from the beginning, pretending he was the guard to keep the crazy people away. Something about his size, muscles, and confident steady demeanor. My eyes get hot, and I chug my wine.

Winnie hands me the bottle, and I empty it into my glass. "Oops, didn't mean to take it all." I go to pour half my glass into hers, but she covers her glass.

"I'm good," she says with a laugh. "Tell me why you think Sean doesn't believe in you."

I take a deep breath. "Okay, I was upset about not getting the part. I was so close. They flew me out to LA and asked me to stay for a final callback, down to just five of us. I connected with the director, with the part, everything. It seemed like this was going to be it. Then I didn't get it. And, yeah, I need to grieve that, and I was having a bit of an existential crisis over why I'm putting myself through all this rejection and uncertainty and just *complete misery*."

"Like you do."

"I know. I get like that when it's a close one, but I really, really thought this was it, and it hit me harder than usual."

"And he wasn't supportive?"

"He was too supportive! He's like, move in with me, let me take care of you. You can keep up your little non-career and always have me to lean on. Like he never thinks I'm going to have a real career. Like I need a man to take care of me! I've always been independent and make do for myself."

"Oh, Josie."

"What?"

"He never said anything like that to me."

I lift a palm. "Exactly! Because you have a great job in the art gallery. He said, and I quote, 'I should quit my job to travel with you because you might get something in a year or five?' Or something like that. I'm paraphrasing. The point is —" I jab a finger in the air "—obviously he doesn't believe in me. I'm a pet he wants to tuck in his pocket." And he'd forever see me as incapable, inferior even. I just can't go there.

She crinkles her nose. "Why would he quit his job to travel with you? You mean to auditions in LA?"

"No, to my future job on location for a movie."

She stares at me.

"What?"

"Are you telling me you guys might break up over a hypothetical future scenario?"

I frown, tears welling again. "So now you don't believe in me either."

She gives my hand a squeeze. "Okay, you're reeling from this audition rejection, I get that. But the fact that you say that I don't believe in you tells me you're not thinking clearly. I've been to every single one of your performances in high school and college. I've saved your commercial and your video series on my computer to watch forevermore. I will *always* believe in you, and you know that."

I choke on a sob. She takes my wineglass away and hugs me, stroking my hair like the big sister she's always been to me.

I cry for a bit and then sit up, wiping my eyes. "My eyes hurt."

"I'll get you a cold washcloth."

She returns a few minutes later, and I set it over my eyes, tipping my head back.

"This is a setback," she says firmly. "You're resilient. Give yourself time to grieve the loss of your dream job."

"I will."

"You can stay with me in Brooklyn until the place sells. I'm going to have it staged with furniture, so it'll probably look better if it looks like someone lives there."

"Thanks, Win. I appreciate it. I really didn't want to go to my parents and have to explain how sucky my career is. I want them to think I'm always busy with auditions and classes. Really hustling, you know? I don't want them to think they wasted college tuition on me for a nonstarter dead end."

"Sweetie, they're so proud of you. I don't think you have to worry about them being disappointed. Sometimes you're too hard on yourself. I know you set high standards and high expectations, and I suppose that's a good thing. It gives you ambition and the drive to keep going. You just need to work on believing in yourself."

I take the washcloth off my eyes. "I do believe in myself. How do you think I keep going?"

"You got angry with me and with Sean because you thought we didn't believe in you when you know I do, and he probably does too. I can't help but think what you see in others is, deep down, what you see in yourself. You doubt Sean because you doubt yourself."

I gape at her.

She pushes my open jaw closed with one finger. "Just let

that sink in. In the meantime, do you want to watch *Roman Holiday*? Audrey Hepburn, Gregory Peck, Italy."

"You have to ask? Of course I do. Thank you." Winnie really gets me. Wait, does that mean she's right? Do I not believe in myself? I'm not sure I can get my head around that one. I've spent years doggedly pushing myself forward.

"I'll make us some popcorn. You want to spend the night? It'll be like old times with our sleepovers. You can sleep in my bed with me. It's plenty big. I won't subject you to this awful couch." She stands and offers her hand.

"Yes, thank you." I take her hand, and she pulls me up. "Oh, Win, I always looked up to you. You've always been so good to your little twerp of a cousin."

She smiles, her eyes welling. "You were the little sister I always wanted." We're both only children.

My eyes well too, and I can't manage a word over the lump in my throat that just won't go away. She gives me a hug before heading to the kitchen.

Much later, after the movie and a peaceful no-drama night, I conk out the moment my head hits the pillow.

I wake to the scent of coffee wafting in, and follow it to the kitchen.

She smiles at me. "Good morning."

"Morning." My head feels fuzzy. I help myself to a tall glass of water and settle at her small kitchen table, a glossy white thing. Colin really had a thing for white furniture.

Winnie hands me a mug of coffee, black like I like it, and then sets a box of doughnuts on the table. I lift the lid, and the scent of fresh doughnuts makes my mouth water.

"Omigod, I love you," I say, helping myself to a glazed.

She laughs. "I know my girl."

We eat in companionable silence for a few minutes before she says, "I need to get to work soon. Feel free to stay. Sean says we can move in to my place on Saturday."

I chew and swallow the donut. "You talked to him?" *Did he ask about me?* I wonder if she called him, or if he called to check up on me. I can't ask. He didn't text or call me.

"Yes."

I focus on my coffee.

She goes on. "I told him you were upset about the audition, and he shouldn't take whatever you said personally. It's a quirk of living with an actor."

"Winnie!" I wince and lower my voice. "It wasn't just drama. He wants to take care of me like a little pet who can't make it on her own."

"He cares about you. For him that means taking care of you. I don't think he means it as a reflection of your career prospects."

"Well, he never said he wanted to take care of you."

"No, but my relationship with him was different. I sort of took care of him. That's just my way." She smiles. "As you always say, I'm a domestic goddess. And that's because I enjoy making sure the people I love are well fed and comfortable. Maybe he wanted to pass that kind of care onto you."

I shake my head and instantly regret it. I sip my coffee and have a stern talk with myself about drinking too much wine. Traveling probably made me even more dehydrated. I get up and help myself to another glass of water, which I down at the sink before filling the glass again.

Winnie sets her mug in the sink and turns to me. "I know you feel like crap right now, but when you feel better, which you will, please talk to him. Don't make the same mistake I did, walking out on him. He's worth it."

"You still love him." The words are bitter in my mouth.

She sighs. "Remember what you suspect in others is often what you're grappling with, way deep down, in yourself."

I stare at her, somewhere between irritated and surprised. Do I do that? Am I in love with him despite his sexist, nonbelieving ways? Is it really me who's the big doubter? But no, he still said he wants to take care of me. His vision of our shared future was us living in his world, like my career didn't exist. And I know it doesn't right now, but I do believe it will one day. Soon, I hope. See, I do believe in myself.

She kisses my cheek, grabs her purse, and heads out to work.

~

Sean

The first week after Josie decided to take a step back from our relationship, I kept cool. I figured she'd see reason and come back to me. Winnie explained it was just fallout from her audition rejection. I thought Josie would ultimately thank me for my generous offer to give her a solid foundation and take me up on it.

The second week was harder. I missed her too much. I couldn't sleep. And she still didn't get in touch. I even checked with Winnie if Josie was still around and not off visiting her parents. She was.

And now it's been two and a half weeks since Josie walked out. Yeah, I kept track. Ya know, just like her cousin, she walks out the moment something better comes along. Though this is worse because Josie didn't even leave me for a real reason. She left because she imagined I wasn't on board with her career.

I'm sick of missing her. I think it's great she's an actress, even if it's a completely unstable career. Is it so bad I don't want her spending the rest of her life crashing on people's couches?

Then it hits me. I do see her spending the rest of her life chasing a dream. Chasing it, not getting it. I pull my phone out and click over to her website, watching her reel again. She's talented, and there's no question she lights up the screen. I'm sure I'm biased because I'm in love with her, but still.

How do I show her I'm in her corner no matter what? I go back to our last conversation, replaying it again in my mind. She wanted to know I'd stick close, even if she traveled around for work. She told me she traveled as a kid with her mother's opera career. Her father traveled with them too. That's what love looks like to Josie. Everyone sticking together, everyone following their dream. But what did her father do?

I look her mother up online and quickly find my answer.

Josie's dad was her mother's manager. I don't see how that applies to me. I know nothing about the entertainment business and would be useless as a manager.

I still don't have any answers when I get to work. It's Friday, and I'm determined to figure something out that gets Josie back to me tonight. I don't want to spend one more weekend without her, not even one more day.

By lunch, I've still got no good ideas for fitting into the version of Josie's life where she does make it. That's all she wants from me. To know I believe that version exists and still want to be a part of it. My brothers and I are having a working lunch at a pizzeria. Dylan's going over some stuff I can barely focus on.

And then I hear "donations from local wealthy people," and I'm suddenly alert.

"Wait, back up. Say that again."

Dylan repeats himself patiently. "I was saying I wanna get donations from local wealthy people for the playground and landscaping."

"A lot of wealthy actors live in Brooklyn," I say as an idea forms in my mind. "They'd be interested in neighborhood revitalization."

This could be my role both in my family's company and with Josie. Dylan said before we all needed to find our niche in the new real estate development business. Dylan is CEO; Brendan scouts out new properties. This could be mine. I've already done fundraisers for Habitat for Humanity. Several, actually, and they were very profitable. Energy courses through me. This can work. I finally see how Josie and I can connect long term.

"I want this to be my niche," I say.

Dylan's brows draw down. "What're ya talking about?"

My brothers all stare at me.

"You said before we could all dig in and find our niche in the company. This is mine. I'll oversee the philanthropic arm with heavy involvement with showbiz people. I've got an in, more than one actually. Silvia knows Claire Jordan. It's a job I could do virtually if I need to."

He stares at me. "Why would ya do it virtually when you're right here?"

"Because my girlfriend is a talented actress, and she's gonna make it big."

My brothers exchange looks of surprise, except Jack, who already knew about Josie.

"All in, huh?" Jack asks.

"Who is she?" Dylan asks me.

"Josie Abbott."

"Never heard of her."

"She's not famous yet."

Dylan stares at me for a long moment. "You're my go-to guy. You said you'd be here when the baby comes."

"Maybe you could have two go-to guys. I could step in if I'm local at the time, or one of these guys." I point at the possible candidates—Jack, Connor, and Garrett. Brendan already has his niche.

Dylan blows out a breath. I know what he's thinking. Garrett doesn't have enough experience, Jack fools around too much. It has to be Connor. He's smart and reserved, always thinking. Actually, the more I think of it, the more I think he'd be a good fit.

Jack makes it easy, holding up his palms. "Don't look at me. I don't want Dylan breathing down my neck about what's gone wrong on my watch."

I meet Connor's eyes in silent communication. *You, bud. It has to be you.* He's twenty-seven, not like he's completely inexperienced. He's got nine years of work experience under his belt.

"I'll be your go-to guy, Dylan," Connor says easily. "Just get me up to speed."

I hold my breath because Dylan doesn't respond right away. He always leans on me because, next to him, I'm the most experienced.

Dylan eyes us both before finally saying, "Okay, it's yours, Con. Thanks. Sean, I don't know what the hell you're doing. You're somehow gonna turn two actor connections into a philanthropic base?"

A weight lifts from my shoulders. "It's a start. I can mix and mingle, connection to connection. I've done it before drumming up people to go to the Habitat for Humanity restaurant fundraisers."

"What about the hands-on work?" he asks.

"As long as I'm local, I'll be working hard like usual, and I'll give you notice in advance if I need time away. I just… Josie's going places, and I want to go with her."

"He's in lo-o-ve," Jack sings in a falsetto, and then drops to his normal voice. "God help us all."

Dylan gives Jack's head a shove. "One day, bud. It'll happen for you. Just keep wishing on a star."

Everyone laughs, even Jack.

Jack shakes his head, still smiling. "No way. I'm heading to Vegas tonight with the guys for Sam's bachelor party. I'm in charge of it, so ya know it's gonna be wild."

Dylan gets serious, pulling the older, wiser brother card. "It's worth the effort to get to know someone for more than a hookup."

Jack smirks. He thinks he knows better than Dylan, better than me. We both know what he's missing out on. Something deeply satisfying.

"Dylan?" I prompt. I need to know if he's okay with my plan.

Dylan turns to me, his expression softening. "Okay for your niche. I wanna meet her."

I jump up from the table. "You will. Thank you! This is gonna be great."

"Where're ya going?" Dylan asks. "It's lunchtime. Ya can't quit for the day."

"I hafta get my woman back."

He rolls his eyes, muttering, "All this and he doesn't even have her?" He raises his voice over the noise of my brothers snickering. "I'm docking your pay if you're late."

"Thanks, boss!"

I smile to myself. Now I have a way to be the boss too. I'm thinking director of the Rourke Foundation has a nice ring to it.

14

Josie

I drag myself back home. It's not the same living with Winnie in a staged home as it was living with Sean in the same home. I know it's crazy, but I miss the air mattress, the shared takeout, oh hell, I miss Sean. It's affecting everything I do. I just had the worst audition of my life because I couldn't play bubbly and happy for a stupid yogurt commercial. Why did I freak out that he wouldn't be supportive of my career? I don't have a career.

Still, even as beaten down as I feel right now, I can't bring myself to take him up on his offer to move in with him and let him take care of me. That's just not who I am.

Winnie's been harassing me to talk to him to try to make up. But what's changed, really? He's still deeply rooted here. I'm still willing to travel wherever I can find work. I should probably go back to LA soon. There's more audition opportunities out there. Except some part of me won't let go of Sean.

You know what? If I'm going to be staying here in Brooklyn just because I can't let go of him yet, then I should talk to him. I'll ask him to meet me somewhere public. Maybe at the park. If I see him, and every instinct tells me to be with him, I'll tell him we need to nail down a plan that puts us on equal footing. And if he walks, well, it can't be any worse than the past couple of weeks.

I stop on the sidewalk and text him. *Can we meet at Prospect Park to chat sometime?*

How about now?

I smile, surprised at the quick response. Maybe he's on his lunch break. *Sure, how long will it take you to get here?*

Look up.

I look up to the brownstone, where I live with Winnie, but I don't see him in the window. I shift my gaze, looking down the block, and there he is, a distance away, looking right back at me.

He lifts his hand, looking solid, strong, and steady in his blue Byrne Construction T-shirt, jeans, and work boots. Everything in me reaches out to him.

I let out a cry and run to meet him, throwing myself in his arms. He hugs me tight.

Tears sting my eyes. I didn't realize just how much I missed him until I saw him again. I was so bogged down, and now I feel light, like all of my burdens suddenly lifted.

His voice rumbles near my ear. "That's some reception."

I wipe my eyes and look up at him. "I missed you so much."

He strokes my hair back and cups my jaw. "I missed you too."

"I don't want to be apart."

"Me either."

I smile through watery eyes. "We need to talk though."

"Agreed. Is it okay if we go to your place? It's more private than the park, and it's right here."

"Of course."

He takes my hand and walks me back toward the brownstone where we first met. "How've ya been?"

"Terrible," I admit.

He gives my hand a squeeze. "Me too."

"I feel like such an idiot. Winnie kept telling me just to talk to you. She swears you're not sexist."

"Nice to know Winnie put in a good word, but it's you I'm concerned about."

"That audition rejection threw me for a loop, and everything has sucked since then. I just gritted my teeth through a yogurt commercial. They're probably wondering why they brought me in."

"Yogurt is gross. No wonder you gritted your teeth."

I laugh. "It's not gross."

He grins. "That's what they're trying to sell you with all those glowing healthy people in the commercials. Eat this gross stuff and you can be glowing and healthy too. I say pizza is the answer."

"And takeout."

"And lots of water to balance it out."

I smile up at him. "It sure hasn't hurt you."

He points to his neck. "This corded neck is courtesy of pizza."

I laugh. "You know how I feel about your corded neck."

We arrive at the brownstone, and I let us in with my key. He walks in behind me, and I gesture for him to take a seat on the couch. It's not his couch; he moved his stuff out. This one is a neutral beige couch from the staging company. All of the furniture is rented except for Winnie's bedroom furniture.

He looks around. "The place looks good. I'm sure it'll sell soon."

"There's been a lot of people through here already. The real estate guy says Winnie should have multiple competing offers by the end of the month."

"Good."

"Sean," I say at the same time as he says, "Josie."

"You go ahead," he says.

"I'm in love with you," I say over the lump in my throat, my eyes stinging. "It's been really hard not being with you."

He cups my cheek and kisses me. "I know the feeling. I love you too."

I pull back and wipe my eyes. "Okay," I say in a shaky voice. "We need a plan, okay? I need us to be on equal footing. I don't want you to feel like you have to take care of me. I don't want you to see me as someone who can't deal with my life. I've made it this far, and I'm determined to keep going no matter how hard it is."

His blue eyes are intent on mine. "You remember how Winnie said I was protective, and you liked that about me? I made you feel safe."

"Yeah."

"That's all I was trying to say before. I wanna protect you from the harshness of, well, everything. I wanna tuck you close and keep you safe with me. But I realize that's not the way you need to feel safe. Josie, I watched your reel again *and again and again*." He pauses at my laugh. "And I honestly believe you have what it takes. You're talented; the camera loves you. I believe in you."

My chin wobbles. "Even if I keep getting rejected?"

"Fuck them if the industry can't see what I can see. But I think they will. You'll get that yes soon. You'll be on your way, and I wanna be by your side."

"I like the sound of that, but how? I can't ask you to leave your family business."

One corner of his mouth lifts. "I figured out a way for us to be together long term."

I bite my lip, holding my breath as hope flutters in my belly.

He tucks a lock of hair behind my ear. "I found a niche for myself that could include you and your world. I'd be in charge of the philanthropic arm of Rourke Management. Our goal is to raise funds to build parks and playgrounds with every development. There's a lot of actors in Brooklyn who'd probably like to see neighborhood revitalization. And if we travel for your job, I can meet more actors who might be interested in donating to the cause."

My heart thumps harder. "But what about the construction side? Your brothers depend on you."

"I'd be there too, but I'd always planned eventually to get more into the business side of things. I told ya before I'm ambitious. This gives me a way to branch out and still be with you."

I can hardly believe it. It never once crossed my mind that Sean's path could fit with mine so beautifully. He made it happen because he sees a future for us. And I want that more than anything. I take him in—the sincerity and, yes, love, shining in those blue eyes. I couldn't ask for a more supportive partner. He truly does believe in me.

A slow smile dawns. "And if I never need to travel, like, maybe I landed a local gig, you could still work with local people here with deep pockets."

"Exactly."

I let out a little laugh. Elation fills me, making me want to dance and sing. It's everything I hoped for! But then, a small voice in my head tells me to think of him. What's best for Sean and his career?

"What?" he asks. "You looked like you were about to throw yourself in my arms, and then you got serious again."

My lips part in surprise as it occurs to me he can read my expression as well as I can read his. And that makes me so happy to know we really connect.

I kiss him. "It's okay with me if you can't stay with me for months at a time, as long as we visit. If I have a paying gig, I could cover the cost of travel for you to visit me whenever you can get away."

He takes both my hands in his. "This can work. We'll make it work. Just don't walk out on me like that again. It reminds me of your cousin, and I can't deal with it. Talk to me, break up with me if you have to, but don't just walk."

"Oh, Sean, I'm so sorry. It wasn't like walking out at all to me, and I hate that it felt like that to you. I just needed to take a step back, and then I didn't see how to get back to where we were. I should've talked to you sooner. I really was trying to figure things out." I shake my head, my lips pressed together, my eyes stinging. "And you can forget the other part too. I'm not going to break up with you ever."

He frames my face with his big hands and kisses me tenderly. I return the kiss passionately.

A long time later, I let him up for air. "If I ever make it big, I'll take care of you."

One corner of his mouth lifts. "Now who's sexist?"

My heart is full to bursting. I beam at him, grab him and hug him tight. "We'll take care of each other."

"That sounds like the perfect plan."

He kisses me again and pulls back, his eyes intent. "Will you move in with me? I've got that couch you love plus a real bed. And all the protein bars you desire."

I laugh. "I'd love to."

"Tonight."

I nod, smiling so big my cheeks hurt.

He stands and pulls me up with him. "In the meantime, we've got some catching up to do."

"Oh my God, we so do." I lead him upstairs to my room on the fourth floor. It's furnished now by the staging company.

The moment the door shuts behind us, we slam together in a hungry tangle of need. His mouth is on mine, his hands tugging at my clothes as I pull at his.

Our clothes fly, and we land on the bed, still tangled up together. He rolls me under him, spreading my legs and settling into place.

"Sean!"

He leans down to the floor for his wallet, pulls out a condom triumphantly, and rolls it on. Then he's back, his hands pinning mine to the mattress as he thrusts deep. I moan and lift my hips to take him deeper.

His breath is harsh by my ear. "My sweet Josie."

"My sweet Sean."

There are no more words.

His eyes mesmerize me, love flowing between us, intense and all consuming. Then I'm gone, lost in pleasure, my cry joining with his groan.

He gives me his weight, nuzzling into my neck. I wrap my arms around him tight. I've finally found home.

EPILOGUE

Three months later...

Sean

I'm in Atlanta with Josie, where she's filming her very first movie. I'm so damn proud of her. She's got a supporting role in a movie based on a band that was popular a couple of decades ago. Even though it's supporting and not the lead, there's a lot of opportunities for her to shine. She gets to sing, act, dance, and has her own romantic subplot. Yes, there's kissing. I'm handling it. Not happy about it, but handling it.

The production company paid for a five-star hotel for the cast, where I'm working remotely for the week. It's a sweet gig for me, to be honest. They're filming for two months, and I'm here one week each month and every weekend. They need me too much at work to stay here for the full two months, but that's where we're at now. I'm here for her as much as possible and, once filming wraps, she'll be back in Brooklyn with me until our next adventure.

I've met a lot of cool people and gotten referrals to more people in Manhattan and Brooklyn, who like what we're doing at Rourke Management. They especially like our royal connection. Since my royal cousins already had a charitable foundation, Royal Rourke Foundation, we made an affiliate for the US, Royal Rourke Foundation US, to focus on giving back to local neighborhoods we develop. The great thing is that a lot of the administrative headache associated with a nonprofit is taken care of by their experienced people. The other great thing is that my Villroy cousins can easily contribute to our cause through the foundation. And, of course, I get to be the boss man here in the US. Once I'm in a position to, I plan on directing some donations toward Villroy's local causes too. It's the least I can do for their generosity in teaming up with us. Besides, Villroy is my kingdom too. I want it to thrive for future generations.

Today's the last day of filming with the big finale number, and I'm on the soundstage set to watch. After this, there's a wrap party, and then tomorrow we fly home together. I watch as they run through it five times before the director calls it good. A cheer goes up, and I clap along with the crew.

Josie hugs her costars and then spots me and races into my arms, still in her glittery silver dress, her red hair a wild mass of waves. I catch her and swing her around. "Congratulations!"

She beams and kisses me. "It's so bittersweet to leave. This group is like family to me."

"Then what am I?" I ask in mock outrage.

Her eyes go soft. "You're home."

"Maybe we'll have our own family one day."

"Sean! You're so sweet. Yes, I'd love that."

"Glad to hear it. That makes this less awkward." I drop to one knee and hold up a diamond ring.

She lets out a high-pitched squeak that has heads turning. The cameraman swings his camera toward us. He's filming this. Why not?

I take her hand. "Josie, you are my heart, my love, and my home. I will love you and care for you for the rest of my life. Will you marry me?"

Her eyes well. "Yes!"

She grabs the ring, slides it on, and throws herself at me,

nearly knocking me down. I rise with her in my arms and kiss her with all the love in my heart.

The cast and crew applaud, and she breaks the kiss, her eyes wide. She turns and throws her arms up in a V of victory. Funny thing is, Josie never was a cheerleader. That's just her natural enthusiasm. "We're getting married!"

"We know!" several people say back in unison, grinning at us. A chorus of congratulations follow.

Champagne is passed around at my signal. I ordered it as a celebration for the end of the movie and the beginning of our life together. I was that sure of her yes. She's so affection-ate, so loving, and so grateful that I'm fully on board with her career. She basically adores me night and day, and I love every minute of it. I've never loved anyone more. I almost want to thank Winnie for leaving me because it brought Josie into my life. Plus Winnie let me stay on and finish renovating the house I fell in love with. It really was a labor of love, at times a headache, but ultimately immensely satisfying. Winnie is happy for us and has already said she'd be thrilled to have me as part of the family. Probably helps that she met someone recently, a sculptor, who she says is really grounded. I think it's great. Winnie needs a grounded guy. And I need Josie.

Josie beams at me and clinks her plastic champagne flute against mine. "To us!"

"To us." I go to sip when she stops me.

"Wait! We have to do the twist around, and I give you the sip and vice versa." Her eyes dance merrily. "Romantic moment!"

She wraps her wrist around mine, and we tip the glasses to sip. She's always declaring romantic moments. Sometimes it feels like she's directing our real-life rom-com. Fortunately, I'm into it.

"I found the perfect place for us," I tell Josie after our toast. Everyone is milling around, celebrating the end of film-ing. "I put an offer in this morning. I'll show you when we get back." She put house hunting in my jurisdiction since I know

Brooklyn, housing value, and signs of a well-constructed home.

She bounces on the balls of her feet, her blue eyes glowing. "Is it in Park Slope where we met?"

"Yes. And it's a bit of a stretch financially, but—"

She goes on tiptoe and whispers in my ear, "I'll pay for it."

I shake my head. "I'll take care of it. My offer rests on me—"

She throws her arms around my neck and kisses me, cutting off my brilliant offer. I let her, enjoying her uninhibited passion. The woman is legit crazy for me.

She breaks the kiss and takes a step back, her expression serious. "Okay, now what did we talk about regarding our future?"

I know, but it's difficult for me. I love her. I want to take care of her if it's at all in my power, and this is.

I barrel on. "Listen, I made a brilliant offer, which lets the owners off the hook for the repairs I pointed out the brownstone needs and gets me in there just a bit out of my price range. I know I can fix the place up perfectly. I got this."

She smiles sweetly. "Sean?"

I let out a breath. "Yes, Josie."

"Remember how we take care of each other? It's not a strain for me now, and I want roots in Brooklyn with you, even if we travel. So I'm covering it, end of story. And you know what you can take care of for me?"

I can't help my smile. I love this woman so damn much, and she gets that I need to do something for her. I can't just let her do all the giving for me, which she does all the time. I've never met someone so generous. She always, always makes that extra effort. She still folds my napkin in a diagonal and pours water for me every meal. (I don't trust her with hot beverages. Thank God she's not a waitress anymore. Liability nightmare.) Plus, there's her generosity with her affection, her compliments, her open eagerness to do anything I want in the bedroom and out. She's a dream come true. She really is.

I pull her close. "What can I take care of for you, my fiancée and soon-to-be loving wife?"

She beams her sunshine smile, and my chest swells. "You can make us a theater room so we can cuddle on the couch and watch our favorite rom-coms together."

I lean down to her ear. "Shh, don't let that get out."

She laughs and pulls back enough to look up at me, her eyes sparkling merrily. "Sometimes I feel like we're living our own private rom-com."

I knew it! I grin. "We'd probably break into song about now."

She pulls away and does a little wiggle. "Or dance."

I give her a slow, sexy smile. "Even better would be fade to black as we walk into the bedroom."

"I like that one best," she says before throwing her arms around my neck and kissing me passionately.

I scoop her up, cradled in my arms as we walk out of the soundstage and into the sunset for our special fade-to-black moment.

Don't miss the next book in the series *Rogue Rascal*, where Jack heads to Vegas and ends up married to his best friend's little sister!

Jack

I'm the good-time guy, so when my best friend asked me to be in charge of his bachelor party, you better believe we're heading to Vegas. After our wild night, I wake up in a strange hotel room wearing a gold band on my finger. Worse, there's a bridal veil on the nightstand.

Then I relax. *Ha-ha. Very funny, guys.* I'm the king of pranks, and my friends are getting me back.

But then my bride appears, and the real nightmare begins. It's Riley, my best friend's little sister, looking all grown up and—gulp—married. To me. My best friend forbid me even *looking* at her on account of my rep for one-nighters.

This has to end right away.

Only somehow I get more and more tangled up in her life, trying to do damage control, and a funny thing happens on the way to ending this marriage—

I'm having second thoughts.

Sign up for my newsletter to be emailed when *Rogue Rascal* releases at kyliegilmore.com/newsletter

ALSO BY KYLIE GILMORE

Happy Endings Book Club Series

Hidden Hollywood (Book 1)

Inviting Trouble (Book 2)

So Revealing (Book 3)

Formal Arrangement (Book 4)

Bad Boy Done Wrong (Book 5)

Mess With Me (Book 6)

Resisting Fate (Book 7)

Chance of Romance (Book 8)

Wicked Flirt (Book 9)

An Inconvenient Plan (Book 10)

A Happy Endings Wedding (Book 11)

The Clover Park Series

The Opposite of Wild (Book 1)

Daisy Does It All (Book 2)

Bad Taste in Men (Book 3)

Kissing Santa (Book 4)

Restless Harmony (Book 5)

Not My Romeo (Book 6)

Rev Me Up (Book 7)

An Ambitious Engagement (Book 8)

Clutch Player (Book 9)

A Tempting Friendship (Book 10)

Clover Park Bride: A Clover Park Short

A Valentine's Day Gift (Book 11)

Maggie Meets Her Match (Book 12)

The Clover Park STUDS Series

Almost Over It (Book 1)

Almost Married (Book 2)

Almost Fate (Book 3)

Almost in Love (Book 4)

Almost Romance (Book 5)

Almost Hitched (Book 6)

The Rourkes Series

Royal Catch (Book 1)

Royal Hottie (Book 2)

Royal Darling (Book 3)

Royal Charmer (Book 4)

Royal Player (Book 5)

Royal Shark (Book 6)

Rogue Prince (Book 7)

Rogue Gentleman (Book 8)

Rogue Rascal (Book 9)

ABOUT THE AUTHOR

Kylie Gilmore is the *USA Today* bestselling author of the Rourkes series, the Happy Endings Book Club series, the Clover Park series, and the Clover Park STUDS series. She writes humorous romance that makes you laugh, cry, and reach for a cold glass of water.

Kylie lives in New York with her family, two cats, and a nutso dog. When she's not writing, wrangling kids, or dutifully taking notes at writing conferences, you can find her flexing her muscles all the way to the high cabinet for her secret chocolate stash.

Thanks for reading *Rogue Gentleman*. I hope you enjoyed it. Would you like to know about new releases? You can sign up for my new release email list at kyliegilmore.com/newsletter. I promise not to clog your inbox! Only new release info, sales, and some fun giveaways.

I love to hear from readers! You can find me at:
   kyliegilmore.com
   Instagram.com/kyliegilmore
   Facebook.com/KylieGilmoreToo
   Twitter @KylieGilmoreToo

If you liked Sean and Josie's story, please leave a review on your favorite retailer's website or Goodreads. Thank you.